THE EYES OF THE DEAD

Other titles by James Chambers

The Engines of Sacrifice
Resurrection House
On the Night Border
On the Hierophant Road

Kolchak the Night Stalker
The Forgotten Lore of Edgar Allen Poe
The Faceless God

Other eSpec Books by James Chambers

The Corpse Fauna Series
The Dead Bear Witness
Tears of Blood
The Eyes of the Dead

Systema Paradox: Devil in the Green

Vox Astra: The Black Box
Vox Astra: When Clouds Die

Other eSpec Books including James Chambers

After Punk
Devilish & Divine
Awakened Modern
The Side of Good/The Side of Evil
Gaslight & Grimm
Dogs of War
Man and Machine
In Harm's Way
Best of Defending the Future
If We Had Known
Footprints in the Stars
Best of Bad-Ass Faeries
Society for the Preservation of CJ Henderson

Corpse Fauna
Volume Four

JAMES CHAMBERS

BRAM STOKER AWARD-WINNING AUTHOR

THE EYES OF THE DEAD

NEOPARADOXA
PENNSVILLE, NJ

PUBLISHED BY
NeoParadoxa
a division of eSpec Books LLC
Danielle McPhail,
Publisher
PO Box 242,
Pennsville, New Jersey 08070
www.especbooks.com

ISBN: 978-1-949691-09-2
ISBN (ebook): 978-1-949691-08-5

Copy Editor: Greg Schauer, John L. French
Interior Design: Danielle McPhail

Cover Art: Glen Ostrander
Interior Art: Jason Whitley
Cover Design: Mike McPhail, McP Digital Graphics

FOR DAVE,
WHO NEVER WOULD'VE READ
THIS CRAZY HORROR STORY BUT
WOULD'VE LOVED THAT I'D PUBLISHED IT.

CONTENTS

THE EYES OF THE DEAD
1

LOHATCHIE CODA
111

AFTERWORD:
THE DEAD WON'T DIE
131

ABOUT THE AUTHOR
137

ABOUT THE ARTISTS
139

OUR LEGION OF THE UNDEAD
140

THE EYES OF THE DEAD

ONE

Inside the crashed yellow school bus, the dead partied.

At least, it seemed so at a glance: a teenage jumble of football, cheerleading, and marching band uniforms, slow-bopping to music only they heard, knocking around a handful of teachers and coaches playing chaperone. They mimicked a wild home-coming party coming off the high of homemade speed from a punch bowl spiked by the school science nerd. Then they saw me, Della, and Christopher stepping out of our Toyota Camry. As if a silent, invisible DJ doubled the beat and pumped up the volume, they thrashed at the windows and rocked the bus.

"Party bus from hell," I said.

"You think they were coming or going?" Della said.

"Hmm, let's say, coming home."

"Okay, Cornell, but did they win or lose?" Christopher said.

"Let's give them the win. Figure they checked out on a high note."

"Could they have been trapped in there from the start of the dead plague?" Della said.

"Safe bet, looking as intact as they do," I said.

"Sucks for them," Della said.

I slapped a hand against a bus window. The dead boogied down for me.

Clustered against the glass, they bared blackening teeth and stared at me with dozens of impossible eyes, the eyes of lost souls that never belonged to those cold bodies. They watched from every limb and wrinkle of exposed flesh, a winking pox. I used to pity the dead, raised up and filled by those invading eyes full of hate and envy. After so many hundreds of miles and months of living in this rotten world, after standing up over and again to the glare of those eyes, of them watching me fight for my life, I couldn't muster an ounce more of sympathy.

I waved my hands in the air and yelled, "Like you just don't care!"

It drove them wild.

"Maybe we shouldn't mess around with them," Christopher said.

Only twelve years old, his voice carried a layer of fear. Dirty blond and with a lanky build that would bloom into muscles in a few years, he put on a brave face, but horror remained fresh in his eyes, deepened by the reminder that the future he should've grown into no longer existed. The young adapt fast, yeah, but they feel things more acutely than grown-ups, especially the thick-skinned criminal kind like me or an ex-prison nurse like Della. Christopher had survived his own hell before we met, lost his entire family to the dead, but a light still burned in him, and I never wanted to be the one who dampened it.

"Don't be nervous," Della said. "They aren't getting out of that bus."

"No, he's right," I said. "We shouldn't push our luck. Good call, Christopher."

He smiled at me, anxious but a little proud.

The wreck had stopped us dead in our path.

The bus blocked the lanes on our side of the highway, part of a line of piled-up vehicles that stretched from shoulder to shoulder and clogged up the oncoming lanes, too, leaving no way to pass. The bus lay tilted about forty-five degrees on its side, propped on a BMW crushed under it. The twisted metal of the Beemer blocked the front door. A smashed Lincoln kept the dead from escaping by the rear emergency door. A street-lamp toppled in the collision pinned shut the rooftop exit hatches. Thick windows held but trembled in their frames as the dead surged against their glass.

All their hungry eyes focused on us. So many eyes peering out from every inch of their exposed dead flesh. Their stares burned with a critical mass of resentment and violence wrapped up smack in our path and packaged inside what, in the old, living world, would've been a microcosm of the next generation's promise.

A breeze tickled the overgrown roadside grass. Empty blue sky sprawled above us.

The air reeked of the dead. No signs of the living anywhere—except for us.

Right then, a familiar, deep bark rattled in the back of my mind. The cackle of my old pal and constant companion, the jackal waiting somewhere in the world to claim me the way death claims us all one day. His breath blew hot across the back of my neck as it had so many times before when he crept up from the depths of my subconscious to remind me of my mortality.

"Shit, we have to make a way through," I said. The jumble of torn metal and machinery hung together like a house of cards with no obvious move that wouldn't upset the pile that sealed the school bus.

"We should double back and find another way." Della wore jean shorts and a navy blue tank top, and the breeze plucked at her silky, black hair, sweeping it across her shoulders and the back of her neck. "Better not to fool with this mess."

We'd fled crowds of the dead together for longer than I liked to remember. On the road, wormfeeders turned to give chase when we raced by, but, slow as they were, they'd never catch up to us on the move. Turning back meant driving into the thick of them.

I shook my head. "We go forward. Christopher, drag Birch out here. We need his help."

Christopher jogged to the Camry and opened the rear passenger-side door. Fascinated by the dead on the bus, Della stepped into the glare of hundreds of eyes that watched us from hands, arms, necks, foreheads, even from tongues visible on one whose lower jaw had rotted out.

I knew more about those eyes than most, but I still didn't understand the phenomenon of the disembodied dead returning from insubstantial limbo to reanimate rotten flesh. Not why it had happened or what it meant.

The dead pressed together on one window by Della, decomposing bodies a single, writhing mass—until, with a sharp snap, a hairline fracture cracked the glass.

Della jumped back.

"Shit."

"Get away from there, Della," I said. "Don't rile them up."

The rooftop hatches bumped and clanked against the lamppost as dead hands shoved at them from inside.

"Why do they have so many damn eyes?"

I met Della's gaze for a moment, then shrugged and looked away. I knew one possible answer to the question, but until I believed it myself, I wouldn't ask anyone else to do so either.

"They're hardened," Della said. "Flesh cured, like leather. Mummified, like."

"They haven't been out in the elements or fighting with the living. It's a soft life on the school bus, all those cheerleaders with their pom-poms to keep your spirits up," I said.

Della smirked. "Wise-ass."

"You're right, though. Thank your nurse's eye for that. I've seen so many of these things, I can't make heads or tails of them but to keep my distance."

"That ought to be enough until we get where we're going," she said.

Lohatchie. The town on the edge of the Everglades where I grew up, where I kept a cabin hidden outside that forgotten scrap of civilization. I hoped no one, dead or alive, would ever find us once we settled in there.

Christopher returned with Birch, a former soldier turned microbiologist, who resembled a ghost—gray-haired, gaunt, eyes fixed on sights only he saw, his black cargo pants stained with mud and blood, but the Hawaiian shirt we'd found him clean and bright. His uncombed gray hair resembled a patch of dead weeds. He'd done no more than stare at us and nod or shake his head for days since he and I escaped a place called Deadtown.

"It's going take all of us to fix this mess, Birch," I said, "See the Buick sitting sideways against the bus?" Birch nodded. "That's the only car not tangled up with another vehicle. It's on the far side of the bus, which means we can push it out of our way, clear a path. The catch is the lamppost pinning shut those emergency exits is resting on its trunk. We have to heft that off there before we can move the Buick, which means we risk those hatches popping open and releasing the teen spirit brigade."

"Why don't we tie them shut?" Christopher said.

"Nothing there to tie onto," I said. "All the hardware's inside. Outside is smooth and aerodynamic."

"Can we shove something else up onto them?" Della said.

"Won't need to if we move fast," I said. "It'll take all four of us to lift the post, but if the Buick rolls, Birch and I can push it clear. Once we move the post, you and Christopher hop into the Camry and drive right up to the opening. Birch and I will jump in. We'll be gone before that dead quarterback can call a play."

"I don't like it," Della said.

"Neither do I, but that's how it's got to go."

Della frowned. Christopher, I give him credit, kept quiet and listened.

"Birch, you in?" I said.

One nod. I studied his eyes, worried he might flake, but I saw enough of the old, scotch-swilling, mad-scientist Birch there to trust him for this.

I inspected the Buick for the dead and found it empty. Reaching through the broken glass of the driver's side window, I put the car in neutral and hoped for the best. At least none of the damaged parts looked like they'd interfere with the tires.

"Everyone grab some lamppost," I said.

We spread out, Birch and I along the length laying on the school bus, Della next, then Christopher at the top, the light itself embedded in the Buick's trunk. Everyone gripped, then I counted down from three, and we pulled. The damn thing refused to budge. Our second try came no closer to freeing it.

"Christopher, you got the light end there, kid. What's happening?" I said.

"The metal's wedged into the lamp, kind of hooked on, but I see how to get it loose now. Give it another try, okay?"

I counted three again. We put our muscle into it. With a broken steel moan and a shattered glass tinkle, the lamp jolted loose. The weight of it shifted to our hands, heavier than expected, but we eased it clear. The bus hatches rattled like loose shutters in a hurricane. We strained and lowered the lamppost to the ground.

Della screamed: "Wormfeeders!"

From the near shoulder, a group of the dead emerged from the brush, all their hate-filled eyes sighted on us.

TWO

"Della, Christopher, back to the car," I said.

"We're not leaving you to fight them alone," Della said.

"We're not going to fight them. Birch and I can handle this. Please. Get in the car."

Whatever Della meant to say next vanished into the clank of one of the bus hatches flipping open. Dead hands pushed through and groped for freedom. The second hatch opened. More dead shoved out into the fresh air. Another group of roaming wormfeeders appeared on the far shoulder, rambling toward us like our voices summoned them from a deep sleep in the roadside brush.

"Are you kidding me?" Della shouted.

"The car, Della. Please. Go. I've got this," I said.

Trusting her to trust me, I tugged Birch along to the Buick, and we set to pushing it. The car refused to budge.

"Damn it, Birch, put some muscle into it, you stringy old bastard."

He hunkered down, planted his feet, and threw his weight against the car. It rocked on its tires. Out of sight, the Camry doors slammed shut. My unwanted friend who lived deep in my head, my jackal, snickered in my ears as death approached. He breathed a hot gust down my collar. I pled with my eyes for Birch to push harder and saw the first signs of real life there in days. We nodded in unison three times then shoved again. The Buick rolled.

"Yeah!" I shouted.

The car moved smoother with each step we took. Three, four, five, six steps, then I stopped counting as the front tires reached the slight incline toward the center median and gravity took control. Birch and I jogged along to keep the hunk of metal and plastic moving until it slipped out of reach. It crossed the left-lane shoulder, knocked down a pair of wormfeeders scrambling onto the pavement, and then bumped to a stop on the overgrown median.

The path for the Camry gaped clear—except for wormfeeders.

The two roadside groups shuffled in our direction. The bus crew learned to let one at a time through the escape hatches. Already four football players aimed themselves at the Camry as two drum majors tumbled out onto the road. Cheerleaders lined up behind them. The dead kept coming. What had looked like a small gang inflated to a crowd with no end in sight.

Birch and I hustled to the space we'd cleared. The Camry came to life and shot forward, bumping aside three decomposed cheerleaders. Its engine noise excited the dead. They filled the road from every direction. Their stench hit like gut-punches. Birch and I gagged on it. If not for the wind, we would've smelled them the moment we'd stepped out of the car and never let them catch us by surprise. Their wordless moans drowned out the sound of the Camry. Their putrid bodies filled the gap we'd made for the car.

On the other side of them, Della stopped and honked the horn.

She screamed out the window, her words lost in the din.

Sit tight, sit tight, I thought, reassuring myself, willing Della to comply.

The dead swirled around me and Birch. We froze.

They came within inches of us, but not one of them touched us. They stared at us; I stared back, wondering who those eyes had belonged to in life.

They lost interest and shifted their attention to the Camry. The bus riders encircled it and pawed at the windows and doors. Birch and I approached the car; the dead backed off and kept their distance, providing us a clear path. We separated, using their aversion to us to reopen the gap. I waved Della through.

She drove clear of the crash zone. I jumped into the passenger's seat. Birch climbed in back with Christopher.

"What the hell was that?" Della said. "Why didn't they attack you?"

"It's a long story. Better I explain while we're on the move. Drive us out of here."

Della frowned at me, then glanced in the rearview mirror, and her frown deepened.

Ahead of us, more dead wandered into the road.

"Now, Della, please, before there are too many."

"Dammit, Cornell," she said. "You and your damn secrets."

She slammed her foot on the gas. The acceleration thrust me against my seat. I scrambled to put on my seat belt as Della wove through the gathering dead. She clipped a few, but it paid to avoid them to prevent damaging the car. They kept coming for almost a minute before open road stretched ahead of us. After a while of easy driving, Della calmed, settled the car into the middle lane, smooth and sure, then spared a glance at me and said, "Talk. *Now.*"

THREE

Where to begin?

I didn't want to keep it from Della. Hated to hold secrets. Only I didn't know how to explain so much of what had occurred in Deadtown. Della and I had forged a bond, running together since we'd escaped a prison transformed into a death house by a fanatic warden. We clung to each other even more after our friend, Mason, who'd broken out with us, died. Then came the mess at Camp Cady, a small, hidden community of the living, where we'd met Birch and Christopher. From there, Birch and I made the trip to Baxtonville, or Deadtown, where the dead gathered in their masses and the strange Red Man who could destroy them or control them with his touch or a thought waited for us. Especially for Birch. Thousands of the dead. Hundreds of thousands, maybe. Of all the living folks who entered that place, only Birch and I left, and the Red Man kept Birch's tongue. Making sense of it proved impossible for me, so how could I have explained it to Della? Part of me still wrestled with the dead walking, that they had a purpose, a resurrection for a reason. Thinking about it at all made me feel like an ant trying to understand a lawn mower as it rolled over my anthill.

Still, I told her as best I could.

"Fifteen, twenty years ago?" she said when I finished.

"Yeah, on a raid because Stradley and his death-torture cult stocked up on weapons, including nerve gas. Birch took part on behalf of the military."

"He shot this Darrell Philip Stradley guy?"

"Twice," I said.

Della glanced over her shoulder at Birch.

"How could someone who died so long ago come back now? Wouldn't he be a rotted-out pile of bones?"

"You'd think, but nope. He's the Red Man, one evil bastard when he lived, and a true-life monster now. Something made him different. When he resurrected, he got up as if he'd died only an hour before. He knows what made the dead rise. He knows whose eyes stare out from their flesh. He's part of why this is happening, maybe even caused it."

Christopher leaned forward between the front seats. "Why didn't you kill him?"

"Don't you think we tried? Every man who went to Deadtown died, except for Birch and me. The Red Man wants something from the two of us. With Birch, it's personal. I get holding a grudge against the man who killed you, but what the hell does he want from me?"

"How'd you two make it out of Deadtown?" Della asked.

"Stradley put his mark in blood on our foreheads," I said. "After that, the dead wouldn't touch us. I walked right through them."

"You figured that would protect you when you sent us back to the car," Della said.

"I hoped it would."

"*Bastard*. You should've told me. I thought you were dead for sure."

"No time for a chat. Anyway, I wasn't sure it would still work. Wouldn't look good if I started bragging then wound up chow for the wormfeeders."

"Hell of a way to test it."

"Got us out of there, didn't I?"

Della rolled her eyes and shook her head. "Idiot."

Christopher flopped back into his seat, jammed in beside boxes of stuff he and Della had grabbed from Birch's lab when they fled Camp Cady. "Is it like he says, Birch?"

Birch raised his head from scribbling in his notebook long enough to nod then resumed writing. He no longer spoke since Stradley ripped out his tongue.

"I wandered out of Deadtown. Stradley took Birch prisoner. Tortured him, maybe. I don't know, and he won't say. We met up later in a grocery store. Stradley meant us to, I'm sure. Let Birch go on purpose," I said.

"It's okay, now, Birch," Christopher said. "We'll look out for you. Right, Cornell?"

"Do our best." I swiveled in my seat to see Birch.

Christopher raised a hand for a high five. Birch squinted at him, then raised his palm and completed the gesture without enthusiasm. I swear the hint of a smile creased in his lips, though, before he resumed writing.

"Shit, we got more dead," Della said.

Ahead of us, the highway stretched long and open, marked in places by abandoned or wrecked vehicles. About half a mile up ahead, though, a line of bodies stretched from shoulder to shoulder. Shadows cast by the high sun hid the details, but the way they moved left no mistake. A wall of corpses crept toward us. They reminded me of when people in search parties link arms and move together, one giant, organism scouring the earth in their path for missing kids or dead bodies.

"Can we drive through them?" Della said.

The line looked at least four or five bodies deep, maybe deeper.

"We'd get stuck then surrounded," I said.

"Don't say we have to turn back," Christopher said.

"Back to what?" I said. "We got the dead behind us too. Only escape is to keep heading for Lohatchie. We keep moving southwest."

"Guess we take the exit then," Della said.

Between us and the oncoming dead, an exit ramp offered an alternate route. We stuck to the highway because sideroads and backstreets came with more blockages—and more places for the dead to hide. But I saw no other option.

"Yeah, let's do it," I said.

Della drove us away from the dead. The exit spilled us onto a two-lane road heading east, nothing around but sawgrass and trees. A U-turn directed us west again. Ten minutes later, we passed a gas station. A fast-food joint came next. Then a strip mall. Soon we rolled into a proper town with shops and buildings lining Main Street. Except for me and Birch in Deadtown, none of us had seen anywhere but the road or Camp Cady, tucked out in the woods, for a long time.

Della slowed the car to a crawl. Even Birch set down his pen and looked.

I don't know what I or the others hoped to see, but the instinct to seek life still kicked within us. That urge, after a long drive, when you first come into a civilized place, to search for the familiar, to orient yourself, and size up the people and places around you. Like a dead phone line, though, the town created expectations doomed to remain unfulfilled.

Della stopped the car. "Gun shop over there," she said. "Grab some goodies?"

"Maybe." I rolled down my window. Engine noise from our idling car. Birds singing in the trees amidst the rustle of leaves. No other sounds. "I don't hear the dead."

Christopher rolled his window down too. "Sounds clear. Not too much stink either."

I twisted around in my seat. "What do you think, Birch?"

Birch lifted his gaze from his notebook for a few seconds, then resumed writing.

"Gotcha," I said. "Thanks for your helpful input, Birch."

Della placed her hand on my arm. "Cool it. He needs time."

"He can have all the time he wants once we get to Lohatchie," I said. "Pull up in front of the store."

The Camry slid in at the curb, and Della killed the motor. The shop looked intact, front door shut, windows unbroken, not an item out of place in the meticulous storefront display of hunting and fishing gear. In the door hung a sign: "Closed. Please call again." The neighboring shops looked fine too, as if nothing bad ever happened in this town, and it had died in its sleep of natural causes. It looked like the perfect illusion of a town. A mask of life.

"Mayberry," Della said.

"Bedford Falls," I said.

Christopher frowned, confused. "What?"

"Like the dead never touched here," I said.

"How can that be?" Della said.

I scanned the street then climbed out of the car. Off to the south, the top of a Ferris wheel crested a line of trees. A traveling carnival. I called Della and Christopher out of the car.

"Think everyone was down there when the dead hit?" I said.

"At a carnival?" Della said.

"Small town like this? Sure. They all went for some excitement."

"Think they're still there?" Christopher said.

"Yeah, I do, or at least nearby," I said. "Smell that? We're getting too used to it, taking it for granted, but there's death and rot in the air."

Christopher sniffed a long breath through his nose, then frowned. "Ugh, wormfeeders."

"Let's make this quick."

I tried the gun store door, locked, of course. I rummaged a hammer out of the tools in the Camry's trunk, wrapped an old shirt around my hand and forearm, and took a whack at the door window. It shimmied in its frame. Another blow. It thumped but didn't break. My blows hit too close to the center of the tempered glass. Planting my feet, I put all my strength into a whack at the upper corner, and the glass cracked. Splinters flew back at me. Another strike. The upper portion of the door shattered. I knocked broken glass free until I could reach in, unlock it, then swing it open. I closed my eyes and counted to ten to prepare for the interior gloom, then stepped over the litter of glass. After a look around, I swore. Someone had emptied the place and not too recently, judging by the dust gathered on the displays. Figure the proprietor saw the writing on the wall when the first reports of the living dead hit the news, quietly packed out his inventory, then ran for the hills.

Della called me from outside: "Cornell!"

I left the store. "Someone beat us to it. Damn place is picked clean."

"Forget that," she said. "Look!"

My gaze followed where she pointed: a white church with a tall steeple down at the far end of the road. The double doors of its entrance hung wide. Wormfeeders streamed out. Even at that distance, I saw their sights set on us. Okay, so what? We had a car, and they were too far to catch us. Even as I formed that thought, a chorus of moans came from the direction of that Ferris wheel as the vanguard of another dead mob appeared on the side streets to the south. From an alley no more than a hundred yards away, another line of them straggled into the sunshine.

"We've got go," Della said.

"Sonofabitch," I said.

The few dead in sight posed no real threat, but small groups grew fast into big crowds. The dead had a way of sounding the dinner bell when they saw the living, a link beyond living senses. No point in waiting around for things to worsen.

I jumped into the car. Della jolted us as she made a wild U-turn, then gunned the Camry back the way we'd come. Along the road, more of the dead emerged from the houses and shops we'd passed. The path before us narrowed. A throng rushed us from a side street, stumbling against the Camry, scrabbling at the windows with rotted, gray-and-purple fingertips.

"Hang on," Della said.

She gunned the engine.

Half a dozen wormfeeders clung to our bumpers, door handles, fenders, anywhere they could grab on, dragging themselves along the road, weighing us down. With every bit of speed they stole, I watched more of them assemble and constrict the road ahead, narrowing our exit until I thought of that Bible adage about running a camel through the eye of a needle, except I was no rich man, and heaven didn't wait on the other side—only the way out of town.

More wormfeeders grabbed on as others dropped off.

The engine screamed against their weight.

"We're not going to make it," Della said.

FOUR

"Stop the car," I said. "Stop!"

"No way! We stop, we're done." Christopher thrust himself between the front seats. "There are too many."

"Trust me. It's the only way we get out of here."

"What the hell are you talking about?" Della said.

"They don't know who's in the car," I said.

"I don't think they give a good goddamn," Della said.

"They will when they see me and Birch."

Birch tugged Christopher into the backseat and leaned forward in his place. He tapped his forehead, showing Della the spot where the Red Man had placed his now invisible mark.

"What if it doesn't work this time?" she said.

"We're goners either way." Our speed slowed to a crawl. More dead surrounded us. Their wordless moans filled our ears, making my point for me. "It can't hurt to try."

Della slapped the steering wheel. "I hate these fucking wormfeeders." She lifted her foot off the gas. The car ground to a halt.

The dead covered it like beetles scrambling over a scrap of taffy, like maggots on a dead bird. I opened my door a crack then shoved. Birch did the same. I figured he sized things up the same way I did. Good. That meant at least some spark of the will to live still flickered inside him. The dead weighed against our doors. We cracked them open and shoved until rotting hands yanked them wide and groped for us. They dragged me from the car, leaned over me with their slack-jawed mouths full of broken teeth protruding from gray, melted-cellophane gums. Then their touch fell away. Their many eyes glared at me and Birch with unwelcome recognition. As I'd done far too often of late, I stared right back.

I picked myself up from the pavement and stepped forward; the dead retreated.

Another step. They backed off farther.

Birch followed my lead. Those clinging to the car let go and slunk away on limbs shredded by road rash. Not far, but they emptied the road east, a channel lined by corpse-spectators waiting for a parade. Word traveled, but only in one direction. Behind us remained a solid sea of dead flesh. My personal jackal laughed; the sound echoed through my head.

"Guess the Red Man still has plans for you and me," I said to Birch.

Birch frowned and flipped his middle finger at the dead.

"Yeah, right, fuck the dead, fuck the Red Man."

We dropped back into the car, shut the doors. I slouched in my seat.

Della stared at me, and I didn't meet her gaze.

"Well, go on. They won't stop us now," I said.

She put the car in gear and drove. The dead made no move against us.

Their myriad eyes only watched. Eyes connected to the dead, linked to a force out in the universe, full of rancid bitterness and concentrated hate, and headed our way in its full fury and malice. The Red Man had shown me that much in Deadtown even if I didn't understand it.

Soon we passed the last of the wormfeeders. Della floored the gas. The Camry shrieked and shot down the road, leaving them all behind. No one spoke until we reached more dead, a few hundred, maybe, blocking our road, leaving us only one way to continue, a direction we didn't want to go: north. We took the turn anyway.

"I swear I saw some of the same wormfeeders from back in that town," Christopher said. "A guy with John Deere cap. A lady in a Prince T-shirt. Anyone else see them?"

"Those ain't exactly uncommon items," I said.

"They looked the same. Same faces, same pieces rotted away. No one else noticed?"

I shrugged. "Like it says in that old vampire book, kid, the dead travel fast."

"What the hell does that mean?" Christopher said.

"Means the living travel slow," Della said. "We've been driving all day, and we haven't hardly made any progress with all this turning around bend doubling back."

"Ah, forget it." Christopher slumped against his seatback.

We drove until the sun sank below the horizon. Worn out and wired, afraid to keep driving in the dark, we parked for the night at a gas station and garage. Pulled the car into the workshop, then shut and locked the door behind us.

Christopher raided the adjoining convenience store for food and brought back bags of chips, cans of chili, beef jerky, and bottled water. We ate the stale but edible chips and stashed the canned stuff in the car. Only Birch dared chow down on the jerky. We took turns standing watch and sleeping in a small, windowless back office.

All night the dead ignored us except in my dreams.

After my watch, I crashed hard. I'd slept little since fleeing Deadtown. Partly from being on the run, partly because I didn't want to dream. The night before we entered Deadtown, the Red Man reached into my head and sent me messages and nightmares the way he'd been sending them to Birch since the dead began to walk, and he peeked inside my head while he did it. I hated it almost as much as I feared it. Every time I slept, I wished his touch wouldn't come, but lately, it did more often than not, and tonight offered no exception.

I closed my eyes to find myself on the run, not from the Red Man, or the living dead, or even the police, but from a man with an oversized shotgun and a novelty hunter's cap, like those goofball foam hats sold in sports arenas. He tiptoed through a forest that resembled a watercolor painting more than anything real and took great pains to keep quiet, making exaggerated tiptoes with his shotgun tucked under one arm, the ends of its barrels like mouths eager to spit lead. He walked past my hiding place inside a hollowed-out tree. I poked my head out, saw things the hunter didn't. Behind a thick stand of trees hid a nurse straight out of a Tex Avery cartoon, full of curves and stuffed into a uniform straining at its buttons and seams. A boy hid behind another tree. He held a giant, all-day lollipop and wore a shirt that read "Little Orphan Boy." At a third tree hid a man in a long, white lab coat. His hair stuck out in all directions. A flask bubbled in his hand, streaming vapors into the air. Blood covered his fingers. An overblown, silly-looking gun hung holstered at his waist. The hunter came on, tiptoe after tiptoe, oblivious.

Little Orphan Boy dropped his lolly. It hit the ground with a soft thump.

The hunter stopped, listened, only feet away.

The boy eyed the dirty candy. His face screwed up, and tears brimmed from his eyes.

Foxy nurse tried to shush him. The scientist ignored them both, pulled a test tube from his pocket, then poured its blue fluid contents into the flask. Colors rippled in the mixture, and sparks shot out. A mushroom cloud appeared in the flask, sprouting tendrils of glowing steam. When it settled down, the scientist drank it.

Afraid to see, I looked down and found myself dressed in a black-and-white striped shirt, black pants, and black gloves—a cartoon bank robber.

"Holy hell," I muttered.

Little Orphan Boy lost it then and broke out bawling.

The hunter smiled and stalked him.

The wild-haired man's potion kicked in. With an explosion of smoke, he transformed into a hideous, hairy monster, popping the seams of his lab coat. He snarled, jumped from his hiding place, and rushed the hunter, who aimed his shotgun and fired, but the shot went wild. The recoil hurtled the hunter against a tree. He recovered and aimed again. As the beast-man reached him, another eruption of smoke signaled the reverse of his metamorphosis, and he reverted to human form. He grinned, embarrassed as the hunter raised the shotgun, and donned eyeglasses from his coat pocket. "You wouldn't shoot a man with glasses, would you?"

The hunter's finger wrapped around the trigger.

I didn't want to know the answer. I forced myself awake, snapped upright from the floor, and banged my thigh against the desk, waking Christopher, who slept beside me.

"What's wrong?" he said.

"Nothing. Bad dream. Back to sleep."

He closed his eyes, and his breathing soon settled into a deep rhythm.

I left the office and joined Della on watch. Birch sat in the Camry.

"Can't sleep?" Della said.

"Sleep just fine, but I can't not dream," I said.

"Oh, lord, here we go. We've reached the point in our relationship where we tell each other our dreams. *Oh, Della, what's it mean when my teeth fall out?* Can I just go fight some of the wormfeeders instead?"

I laughed. "I hear ya. This ain't actually *my* dream."

"Meaning what?"

"Someone sent it to me."

Della eyed me, assessing me, smart-ass or serious. "Okay, talk."

I did, and it resonated for her. I explained how the Red Man sent Birch dreams, how he'd started doing the same for me, and how I believed he'd sent this one, delivering a message whose meaning beyond the obvious eluded me.

"He knows about all of us?" she said.

"If he's in my head, why wouldn't he?"

"Think he knows where we are?"

"I think he's herding us."

"With the dead?"

"Yes."

"I wondered why they seemed determined to keep us from going the direction we want but never interfering with us heading north. Chalked it off to coincidence."

"He wants us up there for some reason, is my guess."

"What reason?"

"Don't know."

"Maybe it *is* just coincidence."

I shook my head.

Acceptance entered Della's expression. It hurt me to see it. Acceptance meant giving up hope for a better option. I put my arms around her and pressed her tight to me. She returned the embrace. We kissed. I sat the rest of the watch with her.

In the morning, we drove out and again found it impossible to head south or west, those directions clogged with wormfeeders. Any attempt to plow through them would only jam up the car on their bodies. We landed on a rural route north, no sign of the dead. Coming around a long curve, though, we found something even more terrifying: Fifty yards down the road, two living people stood beside a pair of motorcycles, one with a small cargo trailer hitched to it. At the sound of our car, they turned and looked our way.

FIVE

"Are the wormfeeders starting a biker gang?" Christopher said.

"Doubtful," I said.

"What do we do?" Della said. "Double back or roll up and meet the neighbors?"

"I've never been the neighborly type," I said.

"If we turn around, won't the dead send us back this way?" Christopher said.

"Kid's got a point," Della said.

I twisted in my seat to see Birch. "What do you say, Birch? Go forward or retreat?"

Birch only glanced at me, didn't even stop scribbling.

"Thanks for the advice," I said.

While we debated, the two bikers wheeled their motorcycles into the road, blocking it, and leaned against them as if waiting for us.

"There's the welcoming committee," Della said.

"Could be more of them hiding in the brush or farther up the road." I opened my door. "Stay here for now."

Outside, the steamy air carried the odor of death, less intense than it had been, which suggested fewer wormfeeders in our immediate area. I held a revolver at my side as I walked in front of the car.

"Hey there," I called.

One of the bikers waved back. "Hi."

"Haven't seen many live folks for a while," I said. "How're y'all getting by?"

The one who'd waved removed his helmet, revealing a gaunt, pale face and sunken eyes inside indigo rings. "We're alive. That's pretty much the whole ballgame these days."

"That it is," I said.

"Listen, man, we don't want trouble or nothing. You want to pass by, we'll move our bikes. I just wanted a chance to talk before you moved on. We hardly ever see anyone alive. Thought maybe you've heard some news."

"Nothing but the headlines, and they're all bad."

The second biker removed her helmet and shook loose her dark hair. She, too, looked thin and pallid, wasted, hungry, her eyes dull, expression flat. "My name's Rhea. This is Damon."

I nodded. "Name's Cornell."

Damon popped a hatch on the cargo trailer and reached into it. I cocked the hammer of my gun, ready to aim and fire, but then eased it back home when he produced a bottle.

"Y'all want to jaw a few minutes, I got some single malt to share."

"Haven't had that in a good long time," I said.

"Getting hard to come by."

One of the car doors behind me opened, and Birch emerged. He walked up beside me, eyed the gun, shook his head, and crossed the distance between us and Damon. His notebook poked out from under his arm. Birch took the bottle from Damon, read the label, and smiled. Damon stared at him, confused.

"You want a drink?" he said.

Birch nodded and winked.

"That's Birch," I said. "He's quiet, but he likes his whisky. Guess we're taking you up on your offer."

I gestured for Della and Christopher to hang back in the car, knowing they would cover us if things turned bad, then joined Birch and the bikers. Rhea pulled plastic cups from the cargo trailer. Birch returned the bottle to Damon, who opened it and poured us each a measure.

"Cheers." He knocked his back in one gulp then exhaled satisfaction.

I sipped mine, savoring the taste and the burn. So did Birch.

"The others in the car are welcome to join us. We don't bite," Rhea said.

"Pardon my asking," I said, noticing close up the extremity of their pallor, "but you both look a little, uh, under the weather."

"Yep, got us a cold or the flu or something. Been dogging us for days. Saps all the energy out of you, but what are you gonna do, right? Ain't bad enough the dead trying to kill everyone, naw, here's a fever and some chills to go with it."

"I hear you. That sucks." I watched Birch, and his expression told me the same question pinged around inside his head: *How can they be ill?* It had been months since either of us had seen anyone sick. Birch's research at Camp Cady had found that for the dead time had slowed to a crawl, maybe even close to stopped at a cellular level and that something similar had occurred in living people. That's the simple, explain-it-to-a-bank-robber version. I don't pretend to get all the science behind it or why it only worked on a microscopic scale while the world at large went on unchanged. Bottom line, the effect slowed rotting and aging, retarded cellular processes to the point of making bacterial or viral illnesses impossible to catch because cells didn't reproduce fast enough to make you sick. Damage by invader cells took so long to manifest that immune system cells, operating only slightly faster, wiped out pathogens before they took hold. Maybe Damon and Rhea mistook malnourishment for illness or lied to cover up for some kind of dope sickness. Or maybe things were changing.

"Do us a favor and cover your mouth if you sneeze," I said.

The pair chuckled with little enthusiasm. Standing around talking seemed to drain them. They moved slow, spoke softly, and squinted whenever the sun hit their faces.

"Where you heading?" Damon said.

"Hoping to go west, but there are too many wormfeeders."

"Yeah, they're thick in that direction," Rhea said. "Gets better going east. We're on our way to Miami. Heard word there are other living people there, and a lot less of the dead."

"Where'd you hear that?" I said.

Damon refilled our cups. "Fat Jake. He rode with us for a few days. He'd been there a while but left to look for his brother. Found him dead and decided to go back. We got overrun a few towns north of here, though, and he didn't make it. Bunch of wormfeeders came out of the grocery store we were scavenging. Bad day."

"Sorry to hear that," I said.

"You're welcome to ride with us down that way if you want," Rhea said.

"Might take you up on that. Have to talk to my people," I said.

"Sure, go on," she said. "We're in no rush."

I walked back to the car and clued in Della and Christopher.

"They seem like a threat?" Della said.

"Seem like they can barely keep their eyes open and their feet under them," I said. "Say they got the flu."

"They don't look too tough. We can take them for sure," Christopher said.

I frowned at him. "Take them? Like jump them and steal their stuff?"

"I didn't mean that. Like if they give us trouble, we could handle them. I don't want to jump anyone or steal anything," he said.

"Gotcha. Yeah, maybe we can take them if they give us a hard time. But they're alive, and that means they're tough enough to survive. Don't underestimate them or anyone else we meet."

I scratched the back of my neck, feeling for my jackal's hot breath. For once, it felt cool and dry. "All right, we'll drive with them for a while, see how it goes. We're heading the same direction now anyway. Safety in numbers, I suppose. Maybe there's something to this about Miami. We're seeing a lot less of the dead traveling this way, so who knows?"

I worked it out with Damon and Rhea to follow us. That limited the risk of them herding us into an ambush. They agreed without fuss, relief in their eyes at letting someone else run the show for a while. They rolled their bikes to the shoulder. After a last nip at the single malt, Birch and I climbed back into the Camry. Della drove past our new friends. Their bike engines growled as they fell in behind us, their ghostly faces hidden again inside their helmets.

We drove the rest of the day, finding more clear roads than not, but detouring around the dead in some places and finding alternate routes in others where wrecked vehicles blocked our path. Heading east offered much easier going than west, but pockets of the dead and abandoned or wrecked vehicles still made progress slow. In the side-view mirror, Damon's and Rhea's black helmets reflected sunlight, bopping up and down with the road. When twilight signaled time for us to stop for the night, I saw another dark shape far behind them. A four-legged shadow keeping pace with us, shimmering in the heat mirage rising off the road. A shape out of my mind. Its laugh echoed but only for me. Its breath burned the back of my neck. Then it vanished in a wisp of shade.

"Damn it," I said. "Where are all the dead?"

"Don't complain," Della said. "We haven't' had it this good for a long time."

"I prefer seeing the knife aimed at my throat."

We camped for the night in a fenced-in utility yard at the side of the highway. It held a pair of mobile, electronic road signs, which we wheeled out by hand to make space for our car and the motorcycles. We ate the last of the food scavenged from the gas station mart. Rhea and Damon produced another bottle of whisky, not as good as the first one, but no one complained. Even Christopher took a taste, his first. We all laughed at the face he made as he swallowed it and the sputtering cough that followed.

Afterward, our new traveling companions settled in by their cargo trailer to sleep. Della and Christopher took the Camry. Birch and I sat first watch. Cloudless sky and a waning moon lit the world bright. The night breeze blew around us, sweet-smelling and quiet.

"The air ain't right," I said.

Birch raised an eyebrow.

"No stink."

He inhaled a deep breath, exhaled it in a long stream, and then nodded. He pointed to his ears and shook his head.

"Right. No moans. Can't remember the last night I passed without hearing those fuckers. Goddamn, their voices carry." Tension knotted above my eyes. I tried to rub it away, but it persisted. "Either there aren't wormfeeders around, or they suddenly turned stealthy."

Birch shrugged.

"Used to be I couldn't shut you up." I stood, stretched my back and legs. "I'm not exactly the 'share-your-feelings' type, but you ever want to talk about what the Red Man did to you after things went south in Deadtown, I'm all ears."

Birch looked me in the eye. For a moment, it seemed he wanted to talk, but frustration crushed him as his physical inability to do so collided with his urge to communicate. He made an awful, hopeless face, then flipped me the bird.

"I hear you." I grabbed my flashlight from the ground. "Listen, I'm going to check things out. I won't sleep if I don't see what's out there. Keep the gate closed until I'm back."

The chain link rattled as I shut it behind me. The latch clicked home.

I kept the flashlight off. The moonlight made it unnecessary.

Earth and gravel crunched underfoot as I walked to the road. A hundred yards back the way we'd come, I found nothing but empty blacktop and overgrown shoulder. I returned, passed our camp, and stalked another hundred yards in the direction we headed. Found the same. If something out there meant us harm, it hid too well for me to find it.

I took my time walking, sniffing the clean air, listening for any sign of life bigger than a raccoon. For a while, I gazed at the moon and considered how low we'd fallen as a species, reduced from sending men to walk the lunar surface to scrabbling to stay alive. The visions the Red Man had sent to my dreams showed a cosmic darkness sweeping over the universe, a malignant force ravenous for every life it encountered. A shapeless consciousness of shadow, brimming with hate and anger, and all the rotten emotions that make people the utterly flawed creatures we are. All the burdens of darkness unbalanced by light of any kind. That balance differentiated people from other creatures, our equal capabilities to do both awful and wonderful things.

Our light. Our dark.

Our capacity to choose, to learn. Our mistakes taught us to be better.

Before the dead plague, before prison, I'd held that light within reach with the woman I loved, Evelyn, and both of us failed to grasp it.

Our last bank job ripped it away from us. One final hit of greed and recklessness before we quit, went straight to raise our child growing inside her womb. Two lives ended when bullets ripped into Evelyn. My own life was thrown into endless darkness when I killed the man who shot her and two more in the wrong place at the wrong time. Guilt and grief made me a willing prisoner. *Lock me up forever. Throw away the key, please.*

I deserved it for failing to protect the only lives other than my own that mattered to me in this rancid, corrupt world. I pled guilty to make sure I got a life sentence and not capital punishment. I didn't deserve to die and escape. I needed to feel it for the rest of my days. I'd thought I'd made my peace with it and with Evelyn's ghost, by later choosing to seek my freedom and live again in this dead world, but even when you're okay with grief, failure, and regret, even after you've put them in proper context, compartmentalized them, and moved on, they have a knack of shooting to the surface when you least expect it. Then they wrap their cold, raw tendrils around your brain. They suffocate you, and squeeze your heart, and drag you down into their darkness. In the first true respite I'd known since that deadly day, all that guilt rushed back to me.

The moon and the stars blurred as tears filled my eyes.

They burned down my cheeks.

I stood there, silent, and cried, and stared at the blank heavens and light generations older than me when it reached my eyes. I lost track of time. The moon shifted to the horizon. My tears dried up. I wish I could say I felt unburdened after releasing all that pent-up emotion, but I only felt drained as I returned to our makeshift camp.

Into that emptiness flowed fear when I saw the gate hung open.

Rhea's motorcycle stood outside the pen.

A voice whispered in my mind to stay cool, stay cautious. Every ounce of me wanted to rush in and investigate, but the smart part of me held back, reminded me that living predators still roamed the world, and they didn't stink like the dead or make brainless sounds.

I crept toward the open gate.

Footsteps came from inside the fence.

Shadowed bodies moved around the Camry.

A muffled voice made a frightened whine.

One of the bodies approached the open gate, wheeling Damon's bike with its cargo trailer attached. I waited until the bike and trailer filled the exit then flashed my light at the blacked-out face.

SIX

Damon squealed and recoiled from the brightness. The illumination turned his skin translucent, revealing veins running beneath it. His eyes bulged.

"Where the hell you going, Damon?" I said.

"Rhea, oh, shit! Rhea," he shouted.

I swept the light across the pen. Birch lay facedown in the dirt where I'd left him, red wetness smeared on the back of his neck. Beside the Camry stood Rhea, dragging Christopher, gagged and bound with cord, out of the passenger side seat. Della, who'd crashed in the back seat, remained out of sight.

"Get him, Damon, get him!" Rhea screamed.

A high-pitched snarl grated my ears as Damon charged me. He reached to draw something at his waist from under his coat, but before he cleared it, I rushed forward and planted an uppercut with my fist wrapped around the heavy flashlight to the bottom of his chin. His jaw clacked shut. His feet left the ground. When he landed on his back, I pinned him in place with my knee and cracked the flashlight against his nose. Blood gushed out. He gagged for breath. I grabbed his hand, still reaching under his coat, and found it wrapped around a revolver. Another flashlight punch, this one to his throat. His fingers loosened. I yanked the gun from him.

Rhea shrieked and opened fire, but the car interfered with her line of sight. Bullets whizzed by me. I tumbled off Damon, rolled across the ground for cover behind a low hill. I lost count of how many shots Rhea fired, but none of them hit me, and wouldn't you know it, the second I realized that fact, howling laughter rolled through the night, through my mind, from my old pal, the jackal.

"Yeah, real fucking funny," I muttered.

I lifted my head as Rhea dragged Christopher across the pen. She stopped in the gate, gun still in hand, and knelt to check Damon. He spluttered blood and tried to sit up.

"What the hell is wrong with you two?" I called out.

Rhea fired in the direction of my voice. Her shot went wide.

"Shut the fuck up!" she cried.

I eased my head up to check my shot on her. She spied my movement and fired. Two more shots, both into the dirt mound in front of me, sending a spray of soil and grit into my face—then came the click on an empty chamber. I didn't wait. I sprang up and fired four times. My first two shots went in low, but I corrected and took heart when I heard Rhea cry out and then topple over. Two shots left. I rushed in to finish her off but held my fire when I saw what I'd accomplished. My two low shots had hit Damon in the head and neck. The other two took Rhea in the stomach and lower chest. She lay gasping for breath, her gun spilled out of reach. She lay across Christopher's legs. I thanked the heavens none of my shots hit him.

After taking Rhea's gun and checking her and Damon for other weapons, I yanked the gag from Christopher's mouth.

"Holy shit, Cornell. They wanted to eat me!" he said.

I untied his hands and legs. "What are you talking about?"

"They left Della tied up in the Camry. They were kidnapping me to *eat* me."

"Della's okay?"

"I don't know." Christopher stood, rubbing his wrists where ropes had bitten them. "It was their watch. I guess they knocked out Birch, and I was afraid they'd killed you."

"Go check on Della while I see to Birch."

He ran off to the Camry. Birch's torso rose and fell as he breathed. I shifted him onto his back, and he roused. They'd hit him on the back of the head hard enough to stun but not kill him, a precious bit of luck. Della emerged from the car, walked to Damon and Rhea, spit on Damon, then kicked Rhea in the side. Rhea yelped and hollered, clutching her wounds with bloody hands.

We dragged her and Damon into the pen. A woozy Birch and I unhitched the trailer, then rolled their motorcycles down the roadside slope into the woods, out of reach, out of sight. While Della drove the Camry into the open, Christopher raided their trailer. Then he lurched away from it and screamed.

Unloaded liquor, ammunition, odds and ends such as rope, tarpaulins, camping lanterns, and similar gear circled him on the ground. Inside the trailer, though, lay Rhea and Damon's food stock, fresh meat wrapped in plastic. Human arms and legs, other bits I couldn't identify, even the partial remains of a head, all wriggling and twitching with unnatural life. Nauseated by the sight, I sifted through them, counting too many to have come from a single body. An eye opened on an ankle. I jolted from the trailer, stumbled, almost fell. When I forced myself to look again, more eyes looked back at me from all the limbs, staring at me with naked expectation.

I knew what they wanted. They wanted me to die.

I slammed the trailer shut.

Pointing at the stash on the ground, I said, "Load that stuff in the trunk."

Before Christopher did, I plucked one item out of the pile, a padlock with a key stuck in it, probably for locking the trailer, but Damon had gotten lazy. Rhea glared as I entered the pen.

"How long you been doing that?" I asked.

She spit blood at me. It fell short and landed in the dirt.

"It's not the flu, is it? You look all sick because you eat that rotten, dead flesh."

"Eat the flesh. Steal their power," Rhea said. "They don't hunt us. They don't bother us. We get a free pass."

"Guess you smell like them." I closed the gate then placed the padlock through the latch. It snapped shut with a metal click. I threw the key as far as I could into the brush beyond the road. "Maybe you're already half-dead inside. Whatever it is, at least you won't go hungry for a while in there since you got each other."

Rhea snarled at me, tried to lunge, but fell to her knees, hacking and spitting up blood.

I helped Birch into the car, then climbed in beside Della.

She turned the Camry around and drove down the road, honking the horn twice as we passed the pen. We risked night travel, hoping to leave the memory of Damon and Rhea in our dust. Few other predators I'd encountered left me so disgusted. As abhorrent as I found the idea of cannibalism for survival, it made a desperate kind of sense. I could understand it if not accept or excuse it. But this? No, not this. Eating the flesh of the living dead, eating toxic meat with living eyes that stared at you, hated you, wanted to murder you, flesh that held consciousnesses embedded where they had no business being. Eating poison. Literal corruption. Devouring the perverted version of humanity. Nourishing yourself on the worst thing imaginable a human being could suffer. That reached next-level repulsive, a taboo too horrible to contemplate breaking. I thanked my luck for walking off to scout the road, or else I might have wound up dead, leaving the others for meals.

"They planned on coming back," Christopher said.

"What do you mean?" I said.

"They wanted to take you out tonight, hit the strongest first, they said, then come back and pick us each off along the road. When they couldn't find you, they panicked and decided to butcher me, then follow the rest of you along the road, grab Della in a few days, then Birch, and then come for you, Cornell, when you were on your own."

"Their brains must be rotting if they thought they would get us that way. What reduces a person to that?" I said. "I'd rather die."

"You saw how they looked," Della said. "Like addicts, like that dead flesh altered their metabolism. There's more to it than survival. I wonder if they could even still eat normal food."

"That possible, Birch? Junkies for the flesh of the living dead?" I said.

Birch reclined in the seat behind me, eyes closed, head resting on a piled-up sweatshirt. Della had cleaned and bandaged the bloody bump where Damon had hit him. He raised his head enough to see me, shrugged, and then nodded once before closing his eyes again.

"What a world," I said.

"At least we know, we meet up with any other strung-out, pasty-looking people, we shoot 'em first and ask questions later," Della said.

"Amen," I said.

The road brought fewer and fewer signs of the dead as we traveled southeast, rolling on toward Miami. The air, unbelievably, grew even fresher and sweeter. Wildlife appeared. More birds in the sky. Squirrels in the trees. Snakes. Even a few alligators parked in a canal with their eyes and snouts prodding out of the water. Houses and stores looked cleaner and less broken than most, and we made good time. The rhythm of the road lulled me to sleep. I needed the rest, but I'd have paid a fortune for a giant, steaming cup of coffee to keep awake because as soon as slumber gripped me, the Red Man touched my mind.

I "awakened" inside my head, my body trapped in sleep.

Black nothing surrounded me. My dream flesh ran cold with the chill of the Red Man's touch. A ruby light winked in the distance, a channel marker bobbing in the waves. I approached it, my legs heavy with dream sensation, the feel of trying to run through water. The light blinked out, then on, out, on, out, on, and came no closer, as if a treadmill scrolled beneath my feet—until raucous laughter came out of the darkness. Part of it I knew well, the bark of my old jackal friend. Part of it stabbed my soul, the laugh of the Red Man.

The ruby light erupted into a searing bright sphere. I cast my hand across my eyes and stumbled backward. The light surrounded me. The red intensified. My existence turned crimson, and some immeasurable length of time passed. The brightness faded. My eyes adjusted to shapes and shadows, a world delineated in red and utterly alien yet familiar. As my sight recovered, I recognized Acme Wonderland, a cartoon theme park I'd visited as a kid. Death stained my frivolous memories of it. Charred and cracked skulls littered the fairway. The entrances to all the rides resembled cave mouths brimmed with jagged stalactite teeth. Slowed-down, carnival music played like a dirge. Red light flared and revealed a tower of skulls reaching toward the sky. High atop it sat the Red Man on a death throne. He lounged in his seat like an emperor sated on power. Coruscating red light crept from the many scars on his body. A hundred eyes opened and glared from every part of him, his body a window to the deranged dead. A thousand more blinked open and stared, many searching the vast darkness swirling above as it spread and reached for him. He offered me a paternalistic smile that made me shiver to my bones.

I wanted to scream myself awake but couldn't force the slightest sound from my throat.

Lazy, indifferent, the Red Man pointed in the direction of the park's largest ride, Connie Caribou Mountain. A force outside myself turned me—or held me still while the park swiveled. Who knew how things worked when a dead man controlled your dreams? The Connie Caribou Mountain roller coaster filled the red sky, an architect's nightmare of loops and knots, twisted tracks, and lines of cars racing along the rails at breakneck speed.

Connie and her gang of friends stood at the entrance, each a surreal blend of cartoon animal and actor inside a character suit, but all twice human size and putrescent. Connie's ribs showed through torn patches on her trademark maple leaf print dress, and one loopy, cartoon eye hung partway out of its socket on a bloody strand of optic nerve. Marvelous Moose posed beside her, his super-hero cape and costume pitted with holes. Skulls dangled from his antlers. His own skull peeked out from rotted flesh; his eyes glared livid in their exposed sockets. Foxy Pinewood came next, matted with blood, his fine three-piece suit torn and smeared with gore. Decayed fur exposed muscle and bone, but Foxy's face remained as roguish and handsome as ever, his sly tongue licking his chops. A sheriff's star hung from his suit. A pair of rusty six-shooters dangled at his waist. The motherly Darlene Deer paced beside him, her dress torn. Tumorous, apple-sized growths dangled from her throat and ribs. A fierce muzzle full of fangs replaced her placid face.

Saturday-morning cartoon, sugary cereal binges had never looked like this.

I didn't know if I should scream or laugh.

The piercing bleat of an airhorn filled the park.

Three figures appeared, fleeing from the mouth of the Polly Platypus River Run.

Little Orphan Boy. Mad Lab Coat. Red-Hot Nurse.

I clamped my eyes shut tight, counted to ten, and looked again. Still there, as if the entire dream hit pause while I couldn't see it. I checked myself for my cartoon robber outfit, but I wore only my regular clothes, a hint that I did not play the same game as the others.

The three huddled together, unaware of Connie Caribou's crew eyeing them from the Mountain. Again, I tried to shout, to warn them, but my lips produced not so much as a whisper.

I ran toward them on rubber legs and feet dripping invisible wet cement.

From his throne, the Red Man laughed.

Foxy Pinewood drew a gun and fired. The shot passed over Mad Lab Coat's head. Now the trio dashed to the next ride over, Captain Capybara's Congo Cruise. Marvelous Moose flew after them. The rest of Connie's crew joined the chase. Connie and Darlene switched to all fours. Foxy slinked along behind them. In the Congo Cruise's entrance awaited Captain Capybara, his nautical attire hanging in shreds from his decomposing body, a black tongue dangling from a mouth of overlong, razor-edged teeth.

I managed another step, then two more, a fifth, but drew no closer to the cartoon stand-ins for Christopher, Birch, and Della. Marvelous Moose reached them first and cut off the path to the next ride. The others soon surrounded them. Little Orphan Boy, Mad Lab Coat, and Red-Hot Nurse cowered, trapped.

A hand gripped my shoulder.

With a jolt, I screamed, at last finding my voice.

"Too late," the Red Man said.

He squeezed my shoulder until it ached.

The cartoon monstrosities closed on my friends.

Connie Caribou took the first bite, wrapping her rotting mouth around Little Orphan Boy's arm. Captain Capybara took the second, biting into Mad Lab Coat's leg. Darlene Deer snapped at Red-Hot Nurse, champing down on her shoulder in an enormous, bloody chomp.

"Go ahead, now, and scream," the Red Man said.

I did. My entire body trembled with it.

Then light filled my eyes. Hot air and stale sweat. The ugly, dry taste of waking up.

I banged my knee against the underside of the dashboard and yelped as I fought against a tightness pinning me until I recognized my seat belt and undid it. I sat alone in the unmoving car. A swift push opened my door, releasing me to stumble out onto all fours and dry heave into the weeds of a crumbling blacktop parking lot. When my convulsions ended, I clambered to my feet, steadied myself, and checked my surroundings: a gas station on the edge of an old shopping mall parking lot. Across from the Camry, Birch and Christopher siphoned gas from abandoned cars into our gas cans. Della approached me, concerned.

"We let you sleep. Figured you needed it," she said. "You all right?"

I nodded and squinted against the high sun. "What time is it?"

"Almost noon. We had to go slow in the dark. We passed pockets of the dead. Covered sixty, seventy miles. Best we've ever done, I think."

"Okay, good."

I leaned on the car and reached in for a bottle of water. I drained most of it at a gulp.

"If it keeps on like this, we'll reach Miami this afternoon, no problem," Della said.

What to make of that good news, I wondered? The water restored me enough to notice the clean taste of the air and the absence of the dead's anguished cries. Della offered me a worried smile. I returned it to reassure her while I struggled to regain my bearings and waited for the ground underfoot to feel solid and real. I tried to make sense of the quiet, ordinary morning occurring around me, hoping it could lift me from the terrifying remnants of my nightmare.

A mechanical sound broke the peace.

The grumbling motor of an approaching vehicle.

In unison, Della and I looked to the highway.

From back the way we came, a truck rushed into sight.

SEVEN

"Find cover, now!" I said.

I grabbed two rifles from the Camry then herded Della, Christopher, and Birch behind a rusting bulldozer parked in the high weeds beside the gas station building. I handed one rifle to Della. Christopher already had one slung on his shoulder, the kid always cautious and prepared the way I'd taught him back at Camp Cady. The truck grumbled along, visible through gaps in the mechanisms of the bulldozer. It brought a stench with it, a cloud of decay that rolled ahead, pushed into the air by the truck's motion.

Stains of gore and scraps of ripped flesh covered the front hood and grill, remnants from collisions with the dead. Armored all around with sheets of steel, the truck looked impenetrable except for openings for the driver and narrow windows along the side of the body. Gun ports. An armored car. I'd studied them a long time in my bank-robbing days. Never could find a sure way to knock one over. I understood the appeal of riding behind such defenses, able to crush the dead under the wheels or plow through crowds of them, but I also saw a rolling deathtrap ravenous for fuel, straining under the weight of its shielded mass and forcing constant stops to gas up. Such a motored fortification might breed overconfidence that might leave its driver and passengers stuck high and dry amidst a thousand pissed-off wormfeeders when they overwhelmed its unprotected wheels. Better to move fast, avoid them altogether how we'd done since hitting the road. Never any downside to making a fast getaway.

The truck slowed then crawled into the gas station, bumping over the curb apron before grinding crumbling blacktop beneath its tires. It stopped. Plates slid back from the side gun ports. Shadows moved behind them. People inside the truck looked out. Then they closed. The engine died and clanked as it cooled.

Seconds passed. A minute. Two.

I hated when circumstances forced me to sit tight and wait, to let tension and uncertainty rise while the world carried on in total indifference. Insects flitted in the hot sun. Birds chirped. On the far side of the gas station, two squirrels chased each other around the trunk of a tree. But the odor of death wafted from the truck into the clean air I'd grown to relish, a reminder never to take anything for granted.

The truck bounced and creaked.

The back door banged open. A woman emerged.

Tall and muscular. Dressed in jeans, a khaki tank top, and an equipment vest from which hung binoculars, a knife, and ammunition for the scoped rifle slung from one shoulder. She wore a black ball cap, her brown hair pulled back in a ponytail. Dark shades concealed her eyes. For a few seconds, she lingered at the truck, speaking with someone inside, then she slammed the door shut and walked toward the gas pumps. She lifted the nozzle from one, then, in a quick gesture that almost cracked me up, she pulled a credit card from her pocket, slid it into the pump's card reader, and then pulled the trigger on the nozzle. Nothing came out. I knew the other three pumps would produce the same results. We'd failed with the same trick so often we didn't bother anymore.

When she exhausted the pumps, she looked around and eyed the cars lined up along the far edge of the lot, looking right at our gas cans and siphon pumps and hoses, forgotten by Birch.

I steadied the others, kept them chill.

The woman tensed as she scrutinized our gear. She jogged out of sight on the driver's side of her truck. Muffled voices carried across the distance. The woman walked to the center of the parking lot and crossed her arms over her chest. An unexpected memory burst into my mind, dizzying in its intensity, a recollection of Evelyn in the moments before she died. The way she stood, her confidence, her presence as we worked the crowd on our last, fatal bank job.

She called out, "Hello," and her voice chilled me.

She even sounded like Evelyn.

We stayed quiet and watched.

The woman took off her shades and ball cap. She ran a hand over her head, then undid her ponytail, shook out her hair, then tied it back into a tail. She resembled Evelyn. Not in features, not exactly, but in her expression, in the set of her lips, in the way her eyes assessed everything around her, calm but alert.

"Listen, we didn't mean to intrude on you. We thought no one was here. No one living, at least. I see your gas cans. I guess we have the same idea about fueling up."

She looked the other way, then back to the bulldozer. She walked to the gas station shop, cupped her hands over her eyes, and peered through the window. She tried the door and found it locked like we had.

"We're going to take some gas from those cars," she said. "We won't take it all. We'll leave you some. If you want to keep your head down, fine. We don't want trouble. But we'd be happy to see some living people."

The whole time the woman's hands never moved toward her rifle. She kept them either crossed over her chest or loose at her sides. I'd spent a lifetime before the dead plague judging people in an instant. Good, bad, trustworthy, or a threat. I trusted that judgment always. It had never led me astray. But this woman reminded me so much of Evelyn I didn't know what to think. I wanted to see her up close. Because I sensed she was safe? Or because she stirred to life a part of me that died with Evelyn? I looked at Della crouched beside me and felt a pang of guilt for my traitorous thoughts. It must have shown on my face.

"You okay, Cornell?" Della whispered.

"Yeah, fine," I said, and then, not knowing precisely why I made the choice, "Listen, I'm going out there. I think we can trust her. Cover me."

Della shook her head and frowned. "Stay down until they leave. Let's not risk it."

"It'll be okay," I said. "She's not sickly like the biker cannibals. Maybe we can help each other."

I crept around the bulldozer, my rifle slung to my shoulder, same as the woman, although she wore hers with more ease and confidence.

"Hey there," I said.

She didn't flinch, only turned her gaze toward me and smiled.

"Hey there, yourself," she said. "My name's Vale."

"Cornell."

"Listen, I meant every word I said. My friends and I don't want trouble. We're surviving like the rest of the living. I lost track of how long it's been since we've met anyone else, though. Except for the dead-eater we found back up the road."

"Dead-eater?"

"Cannibals, sort of. They, um, eat the wormfeeders."

I scratched my cheek. "The one you found, she didn't happen to be locked up in a roadwork pen, did she?"

"You know her?"

"I'm the one who locked her up."

"They're gone in the head. The dead flesh melts the brain. Turns them into violent weirdos. It's a mercy to put them down. Makes the world safer too."

"I've never been one for killing in cold blood, though."

A white lie. An image of Evelyn lying dead on a bank floor flashed through my head. Then the flash of my gun as I shot the guard who killed her and two more who rushed me. Ice running through my veins.

Vale shrugged. "Me neither, but when everything wants to kill you first, what counts as cold blood?"

"Long as you don't turn that philosophy toward me."

"The living need to work together. Or at least let each other be. Speaking of which, I'm going to take that gas now. Like I said, I won't take it all. In case you get skittish, you should know my friends in the truck are covering me."

"I've got friends too," I said.

"Good. Keeps it fair."

"You gotta wash that truck. It reeks."

Vale laughed. "It's awful, isn't it? That's camouflage. The dead smell their own, they're less likely to swarm us."

"Where you coming from?"

"Up north quite a ways. The airport at Actsburg. We had a refuge there until the dead overran it."

"No place stays safe for long. How many in your group?"

"Back in Actsburg? More than a hundred before shit went south. Now? There's three of us, and in case you're a numbers guy working the odds, I guarantee no one in your crew is as good a shot as me."

I laughed at her mix of bravado and sweetness. I'd only ever seen the like in Evelyn.

"Numbers guy? Maybe, but not the way you mean. There are four of us."

"Thanks for sharing."

She retrieved two gas cans and a siphon from her truck and then started at the car farthest from where we'd left our gear. Once the first can started filling up, we made eye contact, sizing each other up. I wanted to take the next step in trust, maybe even lend a helping hand, but despite the risk I'd already taken, I couldn't surmount my fear of ambush, or lies, or being wrong again about throwing in with another human being like I'd been wrong about Damon and Rhea. That mistake had come damn close to costing us our lives.

After she filled her first can, she did the second. When that one filled, she carried them to her truck and poured the contents into its gas tank. She walked back to the same car, siphoned it dry, half a can, and then moved to the next car to continue. I watched her the way I used to watch Evelyn when she did simple things like put her clothes away after washing them or get dressed for a night on the town.

Footsteps crunching behind me broke the spell.

Della came out from behind the bulldozer.

"We've got some food if you're hungry," she said.

Vale scrunched her face, unsure what to make of Della, as if she thought we were playing a trick on her—or she had no idea anymore how to respond to kindness.

"I'm Della." She gave the smile she used to put panicked patients at ease. It worked.

Vale relaxed. Her tension gave way to a grin. "Oh, yeah? What you got?"

Della walked over to the Camry, rummaged around inside, and came up with a package of Oreo cookies she'd been saving for a special occasion. I swear a tear ran down Vale's cheek at the sight of them, but I stood too far away to say for sure. Vale waved to her people inside the truck. The doors opened. A man and a woman climbed out with guns handy but not a threat. The man wore jeans and a gray mechanics shirt. The woman sported running shorts and a fleece hoodie.

"This is Dawson and Gordon," Vale said.

I whistled. Christopher and Birch rose from cover.

"The young guy is Christopher. The other is Birch. He doesn't talk."

"Nice to meet you all."

Della ripped open the Oreos. We all dug in. Even slightly stale, they tasted magnificent.

"Where you heading?" Vale said around a mouthful of cookie.

"Long story. Right now, Miami."

"That so? We're heading there too."

EIGHT

We wound up driving down Route 27. Vale's crew took the lead, and we drove in their wake, windows up against the unrelenting awfulness of the odor, but it did the trick. The few times we passed clusters of the living dead, they paid us no attention at all. For a while, none of them showed up anywhere, then Miami embraced us. Route 27 became East Okeechobee Road.

After that, we only saw dead bits and pieces, twitching limbs, or single corpses too broken to move, stuck in place as if the sun had melted them to the pavement.

Around Miami International Airport, the welcoming committee rolled out to greet us.

A red convertible parked in the middle of the road. Two men and two women stood in front of it, one couple black, the other white, all dressed in beach clothes—bathing suites, linen shirts, and flip-flops. They waved us down.

Vale's truck stopped in the middle lane about fifty yards shy of them. Della stopped the Camry in the right lane so we could see. The locals spoke. I rolled down my window, but I still couldn't make out what they said. The back door of the truck cracked open, and Vale dropped out with her rifle in hand. She gestured to me: She would provide cover while I found out what they wanted. For a moment, I froze. Did Vale trust me that much already? Did I trust her? I felt no natural hesitation about her. When I looked at her, I saw Evelyn in my mind.

"Cornell?" Della said.

"Yeah, got this." I swiped a Beretta 92 from the glove box and stepped out of the Camry.

"Hey there," the black man called and waved.

I waved back and walked as far as the truck's passenger-side door. If shit went south, I could drop and roll under it for cover. Best I could tell, though, our greeters carried no weapons, and they'd come alone, not another car or person in sight.

"What can we do for you?" I asked.

"This may sound odd," the man said, "but we've been waiting on you for weeks."

"Waiting on who?" I said.

The black woman straightened from leaning on the car. "On you. You're Mr. Cornell, aren't you? Mr. Birch in one of these vehicles too?"

A warm breeze filled the silence. It carried a sound I'd lived with for far too long now, always on the edges of my thoughts: the jackal's laughter, no less cutting in its mockery of my belief that I controlled any part of my fate. The message came clear: I would never shake free of it. The world wasn't finished chewing me up, let alone ready to spit me out. Who could know me, know which direction I would go? Who could've sent all those dead to herd us down this path to here and now? Only the Red Man.

I pulled the Beretta 92 from the back of my waistband, where I'd tucked it as I left the car, held it low in front of me, ready to aim, to kill. The members of the welcoming committee flinched. Fear livened their expressions.

"You work for the Red Man?" I said.

"No, no, man, you got us all wrong," the man said.

"What the hell does Stradley want with us? Huh? Why does he keep playing with me? He still after payback for Birch?" I said.

"I don't know," the man said. "We've heard of the Red Man, but we don't work for him. We have no idea what he wants. Okay?"

The woman took a deep breath. She stepped forward, calm but frightened eyes darting between the gun and my face. I'd met half a dozen like her robbing banks. Terrified but capable of keeping composed, of navigating a fucked-up situation.

"I'm guessing you're Mr. Cornell," she said. "We don't want to hurt you. We only know of the Red Man. He's not here. He didn't send us."

"How the hell do you know who I am?"

"We see his mark on you," she said.

"What mark?" I said.

"On your forehead. Where he touched you," she said. "The Red Man isn't the only one with power over the dead."

"What the hell does that mean?"

"Listen, my name's Erika," the woman said. She pointed at the man who'd spoken, then at the white couple. "That's my husband, Octavio. That's Denny and Ruth. We're no threat to you. We can't answer your questions. If you come with us, we'll take you to the ones who can. They know better than us what the Red Man can do and what he is."

"If we don't come with you, what then?"

"I really don't know. We were told to expect you and Birch and another, a woman, Vale, and to show you the way into town, where it's safe. Where you can rest without fearing the dead will come knocking any second. We all have a part to play in... the end of the world, I guess, and if you do our bit, things go one way. If you refuse, things happen differently.”

“That’s it? Plans change?”

Erika shrugged. “Yeah. I mean, we can’t force you. You’ve got to choose your own path for it to work.”

“Hey, man.” Denny pushed himself off the hood of the car. “We got no axe to grind with you. We’re here to deliver an invitation and guide you to the ones who have answers. You don’t want the answers? S’okay, cool, we go our own ways, the world keeps falling down this fucked-up rabbit hole of death, and everything turns to dust. That’s all.”

“What kind of answers?”

“The kind you get from a saint,” Octavio said.

“A lot more sinners in this world than saints. Make some damn sense already,” I said.

Footsteps crunched behind me. Instead of turning to see who’d stepped forward, I watched the eyes of our welcomers. Almost as one, their gazes shifted over my left shoulder, and their expressions widened with surprise.

“You got his mark,” Erika said. “Mr. Cornell’s is red, but yours is white. You must be Vale. St. Bianco told us you’d be coming too. We never figured you’d arrive together.”

“St. Bianco is here?” Vale said.

“Friend of yours?” I asked.

Vale shook her head. “Not exactly.”

“We don’t understand all this stuff,” Erika said. “The dead holy folk blessed us, which is why we can see your auras, see the marks on you, but none of us knows how it works. It sounds corny, but we’re taking all this on faith.”

“Come with us, get some answers,” Octavio said.

“Or don’t,” Denny said. “Save the world or let it die. Your call, man.”

“Dead holy folk?” I said. “As in living dead?”

Vale and I exchanged glances. She knew more about this than me. I read it in her face.

“They for real with this ‘holy’ talk?” I said.

“Could be, yeah,” she said.

I squinted at her. “Oh, yeah? You got a lot of saints for friends?”

"Only the one," she said, "and when I knew St. Bianco, he didn't have much to offer the living except staying dead for good when you die. So, what's changed?"

"You'll have to come with us and ask him yourself," Erika said.

NINE

We followed the red Corvette into the big, bright city of Miami. Buildings shone in the sun. Heat filled the air.

As far east as I could see, hazy light emanated from a point down by the ocean and filled the sky. I recalled the crimson glow that had flowed along the streets of Baxtonville, heralding the arrival of the Red Man and death for everyone with us except me and Birch. The dead had ruled that town. Here I saw life. It gave me a tiny flicker of hope I expected reality to snuff at any moment.

The 'Vette led us south and east until we crossed Biscayne Bay via A1A and drove into South Beach. Erika and her crew guided us along the strip. The sight set my head spinning. On one side of the street stretched green grass and beaches filled with people in bathing suits and summer clothes. On the other, sidewalks punctuated by outdoor cafes where people drank coffee and ate, where faces peered out from hotel room balconies and windows.

Living people.

Eating, walking, sunbathing, jogging. Smiling. Laughing.

Going about life like it used to be.

Music played. I rolled down the window. A band performed an acoustic cover of an old Stones' song, "Gimme Shelter," in one of the cafes. The sound faded as we passed.

I hadn't been to South Beach in years. It looked like I remembered it. Alive. Set off from the rest of the world. Clean sand, lush strip parks, and the Atlantic Ocean rolling in on powerful waves. Untouched by the dead. It took more than Biscayne Bay and the Intracoastal Waterway to provide that kind of protection.

"So many people," Christopher said. "So many bikinis."

"Keep your eyes in their sockets, kid," Della said. "How's this possible?"

"Your guess is as good as mine." I twisted to face Birch. "Unless our resident mad scientist cares to enlighten us?"

Lifting his gaze from his notebook, Birch only shrugged.

Along the road, palm trees swayed in the breeze. A group played volleyball on the beach. Another group danced on the sidewalk to a hip-hop cassette playing on a boombox. Our caravan drew curious glances, even looks of disgust as the stink of Vale's truck spread in the air. The aroma of meat and spices sizzling on a charcoal grill drifted into the car. My stomach growled; my mouth watered. The world as it had been before the dead rose, except for little signs of the new reality. People on the beach, yeah, but only a tiny sliver of a fraction of how many would've once been there on a gorgeous day like this, and more than a few carried weapons or kept them propped up against their beach chairs. Men with rifles stood watch on the roofs of the tallest buildings. The inner darkness of the hotels, shops, and restaurants without electricity. The expressions of people who looked upon Vale's truck as if a horror movie had rolled into town, one they'd seen too many times already.

The convertible turned down an alley that connected to a parking garage behind one of the big, old art deco hotels. We followed. I kept my gun in hand. If we'd made the wrong call and Erika had led us to an ambush, we'd only have one choice: fight. But no attack came. Nor did I truly expect one. Something about all this felt, if not right, appropriate, as if whatever lay in our future, an innumerable array of alternate possible outcomes or a single, locked-in destiny, it lay on the other side of this place, a nexus through which we must pass to reach it. The Corvette rolled into a parking space far from the hotel entrance. Denny emerged and directed us to two nearby spaces. All the engines died, and the garage echoed with quiet.

Vale and I exited first, guns ready.

"You won't need those." Octavio pointed at our weapons.

"I'll make that call myself, you don't mind," I said.

"Nah, man, suit yourself," he said. "Trusting us is a lot to ask, I get it."

Dawson and Gordon climbed out of the rot van, Della and Christopher from the Camry.

"Sorry to park us so far from the door." Denny waved his hand in front of his face. "Need to keep that stink away."

"Ready?" Erika said. "What about Mr. Birch?"

I knocked on Birch's window. He gave me a look that said it all, and I heard his voice in my head, the way it used to sound: *Are we really doing this? There's no turning back. Why don't we walk our asses across the street and sit in the sand instead? Soak in the sun and the salt air. Let this rotting world keep rotting and enjoy what's left while we can.*

I crushed his hopes. "Come on, Birch. The bastards in charge here can't be any worse than the bastards in charge anywhere else, can they? So, let's go meet the mayor, even if it's just to tell him to fuck off and die."

Birch cracked the first smile I'd seen from him since before Deadtown. We both had our history clashing with authority. That grin lasted only half a second then vanished. He shoved his notebook into the box beside him on the seat then opened his door. I backed up, gave him a hand getting out, and then the lot of us walked toward the hotel entrance. I whistled that old tune from *The Wizard of Oz*: *We're off to see the Wizard, the wonderful Wizard of Oz.* Only Denny laughed. Octavio and Ruth held the doors. We entered into cool darkness.

Our eyes adjusted to the gloom. We stood in a small lobby that had popped wholesale out of a 1930s movie about big city life. Denny guided us along a corridor where a fuzzy blast of daylight glimmered at the far end, and we traversed it to a vast lobby. Accordion windows folded back along the front wall opened onto the street, permitting fresh air and light to enter. It overlooked a sidewalk plaza of tables, chairs, and palm trees, all with an ocean view. Daylight chased off the gloom, but another light illuminated the space too. A bright organic haze radiated from seven men and women seated in high-backed chairs in the lobby's lounge area. About half a dozen people sat around them in smaller chairs or on the floor.

My chest muscles clenched as I saw how much the glowing people resembled the Red Man, skin almost vivid enough to pass for living, but too dry, too tight. Deep wrinkles around their sunken eyes. Little scars that would never heal or fade. They wore clothes unsuited to their mystical appearance.

Tattered and stained shirts, ragged dresses, torn jeans, no shoes. Their bare feet mottled, black at the toenails. They looked asleep, eyes closed, expressions still. Every few seconds, I glanced away from them, let my sight focus on Della or Vale or the glorious day outside. Looking at them straight on for too long produced an ache behind my eyes that threatened to grow until it split my skull. Ideas and impressions pushed into my thoughts. Voices whispered at the edge of my hearing. Like the Red Man's dream. Invasive species of the mind. Outrage filled me.

My voice, harsh and righteous, cracked the silence. "Get the hell out of my head, you goddamn wormfeeders."

The glow of the dead holy folks brightened. Their eyes snapped open. Dusky, powerful glares, the whites of their eyes glimmering in dark pits. I glared back at them, fed up with staring down dead eyes. The walls and floor vibrated. A low hum quivered the room. The living people in the lounge area and our welcoming committee flinched and cowered. So did Vale's people and mine, except for me, Birch, and Vale.

Instead of shrinking from the show of power, we stepped toward it.

"You want something from us, we're here to listen," I said. "Otherwise, I might like to go crack a few beers on the beach and work on my tan."

Birch, of course, said nothing, but he put on a good show of looking bored.

The hum faded.

The dead holy folk stared a little longer.

The one in the center lifted a hand and blessed us with the sign of the cross.

"Don't take it personally," I said, "but I haven't been to church since the sixth grade."

Dressed in tattered black jeans, a once-white dress shirt, and a black leather jacket that looked like salvage from a motorcycle crash, he stood and took four steps toward us.

"Don't turn your back on God, Mr. Cornell. You'll need all the help you can get."

"God hasn't helped this sinner yet. Why would he start now?" I said. "How the hell do you know me, know any of us?"

He smiled, nothing pleasant in the expression. "Some of *you* know me. Vale. Gordon. Dawson. I trust your road here wasn't too much of a trial. I don't see Ms. Gallegos with you, though, so I gather you suffered a loss. Did she rise when death took her?"

We waited for someone to answer. Vale tried to bore holes into the dead man with her eyes until Gordon said, "She didn't."

"I'm gratified to hear it. May she rest in peace."

Vale's voice crashed out of her throat. "How dare you? How dare you leave the people we knew in Actsburg to die, then you come down here and set up your little beach party, and what—*what* the hell is it you want?"

"I understand your anger," the holy man said. "I did, indeed, show those people mercy. None would've survived, would've lived more than a day or two after leaving the airport where you took shelter. None would've arrived here, now, and stood safe from the living death astride the earth. Only you, Vale. You were the only one I *knew* would live on. If I hadn't blessed the others, they would've risen and added to the strength of the darkness aligned against the living. Do you understand?"

"No, I damn well do not," Vale said.

"Wait a minute," Gordon said. "You mean you thought me and Dawson would die, and you still withheld your blessing?"

"No. I gave you my blessing freely, as I did for Gallegos, then hoped for the best. Had you died, you wouldn't have risen. Now here you are, alive, I'm overjoyed to see."

Birch clutched my arm, gripped it so tight I winced. He looked at me, his face burdened by so much he wanted to communicate but couldn't say. I knew, though. The same terrible idea had formed in my head too.

"Only one other person I know can keep the dead from rising. Only one other person can put the dead to rest," I said.

"You're mistaken, Mr. Cornell. I don't put the dead to rest. I send the living to ultimate peace and remove their fear of rising," he said. "Others hold power like mine—or like that of the man you mean, Darrell Philip Stradley. But while we are many, there is only one man I know of who can send the Red Man to true death forever, and that man, Mr. Cornell, is you."

TEN

Seven living dead saints, holy folks, bodhisattva, prophets, whatever you call them, they set my skin crawling and tied knots in my gut. Their chests didn't rise and fall with breath. Their lips never moved, except for St. Bianco's. Their eyes never blinked, as if an artist had painted them on stone. I couldn't say if I stood in the presence of divinity, spiritual miracles, or simply dead bodies less rotted than all the rest. Flesh with enough brain cells still sparking to pretend to something more than death. It didn't matter.

For all their weirdness and formality, at heart, they were only another crew of people who believed they held the right to order me around, to control where I went and how I lived, to erase my wants and goals, and force their own into my head. Like Warden Lane Grove in prison. Like Sheriff Tom Weichert at Camp Cady. Like the Red Man. Self-appointed. Controlling. Arrogant. Indifferent to the hopes and desires of those beneath them. So unironically self-assured in their divine right to toy with the lives of others, they didn't see how they destroyed themselves.

"You're wrong," I said. "The Red Man is already dead. No one can put that rabid dog down for good except maybe one of you if you've really got the magic touch. Anyway, I've got other plans. You and your creepy-eyed friends can do the same thing everyone else who's tried to run my life has done, and go—"

"Mr. Cornell, you misunderstand us."

St. Bianco's voice boomed. It resonated in my bones, in the lobby walls.

It brought a cold wind that twitched at our clothes and hair.

Everyone, including me, flinched.

The misty glow around the dead holy folk intensified, deepened all the shadows in the lobby, and pushed the beautiful day outside away from the hotel. We stood in a bubble that his voice solidified. The sounds from beyond the open windows dimmed.

"You say we're arrogant. Yet it's you who assumes he can be a savior."

St. Bianco approached me. His body glided, legs barely moving. Energy radiated from him and tickled my skin. His light filled my eyes, entered me, suffused me with a calmness I hadn't known in years, and chased away my tension and anxiety. Even the breath of the jackal panting down my neck faded. His presence in the recesses of my mind vanished, leaving me free of him for the first time since before Evelyn died. All of this occurred so suddenly my head spun, and my knees trembled.

"We've seen many like you on this new dead Earth. People capable of adapting, of carving survival from the world no matter the obstacles stacked against them. People of spirit and willpower. Defiant, independent souls. The seven of us gathered here pooled our energies to repel the dead and create a haven for the living. The societies we knew, the natural order that once reigned, are decimated beyond recovery. A new world is quickening. We'll all witness to its birth. There's still time to tip the balance of things toward life and away from death, but it cannot be assured. Thus, we've followed the lives of people such as you and Vale, called to them in the night or touched their lives on our own journeys. We hoped for dozens, maybe hundreds of them to gather here. People with the spiritual stamina and the psychological surety to confront the Red Man. Since the early days of the dead plague, we've waited for you to come. Do you know many have arrived?"

All around me, confusion filled the expressions of my people, of Vale's, of the four who met us coming into the city. Sadness darkened their eyes too. Outside the windows, a new thing revealed itself. An awful, persistent fear and resignation in the faces of passersby. No matter how safe they felt here in this blessed city district, they knew—and could never forget—a world of the dead awaited them outside the city limits.

"Vale and I are the first?" I said.

"The first and only."

"What happened to the others?"

"Some died. Others broke under stress. Many ignored the greater needs before them and chose only survival in fortified pockets of apparent safety that one day will betray them."

"Can't blame them for surviving. That's prerequisite to everything else."

"Survival isn't truly living. It's scavenging off the corpse of the world."

"Like insects on a dead body."

"Yes."

"Yeah, well, we don't have the luxury of control over the dead like you do."

"You have more power than you think. Why else would the Red Man work so hard to turn you to his side? He's in your head, isn't he? And Mr. Birch's? He knows you're here. He tried to divert you, but he succeeded only in keeping you from going where you wanted. He lacked the power to force you to him as he desired. You skirted the edge of his influence and the limits of ours. You traveled the border between the light and dark, life and death, and your path ended at life. The Red Man sends you dreams because he fears you. He's done this to others. Many of those we hoped would join us turned to his side. None he's touched have held their ground like you."

"So, what? I'm supposed to play high noon with the Red Man? There can be only one? That kind of crap?"

"You're not supposed to do anything, Mr. Cornell. Your life is your own. You have free will like all the others. My sisters and brothers and I hoped for many like you—those who frighten the Red Man—to face him together with each other's support and protection. We wish a better future for the living. Only you and Vale have arrived. If I were you, I'd find those beers and head for the beach. The world belongs to the dead now. You and your companions, like everyone in this city, are dying by the second in a world that wants you only for raw flesh to house lost and angry souls."

The words stung. Was that all we struggled for? The opportunity to die on our own terms, to depart this world the way we'd always figured we would, and leave behind our bodies to the awful, new, unnatural order?

"Something's coming," I said.

"Something?" St. Bianco said.

"A dark thing. I don't know what it is or what to call it. The Red Man showed it to me in the dreams he sends. It's vast, angry, bitter, all the bad things you can imagine."

"We know."

"What are you doing about it?"

"What's to be done? If it is called, it will come."

"The Red Man's calling it?"

"Yes. And others like him. Stradley is only one of those who had a hand in bringing the dead to life. Others around the world have followed paths that parallel his. The details vary; the power doesn't. Others like us and like you exist around the world too. Events similar to these are playing out, have played out, or will do so soon in many places. We can only hope enough of the ones who can make a difference choose to keep that darkness from arriving. Here, at least, we've failed. So why not enjoy the light and warmth, live in the brightness, until it vanishes forever."

"That's not the life I want."

"What life do you prefer?"

Della held Christopher close, her arm around his shoulders. Her expression reminded me of when we first met, when she saw in me only a criminal, a convict, another untrustworthy man for her to guard against. Now she aimed that harshness and skepticism at the dead holy folks. She didn't trust them. Good. Neither did I.

"To be left alone," I said. "To get where we're going and live our lives in peace."

"If peace is all you want, I can provide it now. My blessing will stop you from rising after you die. We have a place here where you can go and the means to make it painless. Others have chosen that path. You can help the woman and the boy first, then see to yourself."

St. Bianco reached for my forehead.

I stepped back. "Don't touch me!"

I threw a punch at him, aiming for his chest, but my fist found only empty air. Without even appearing to have moved, St. Bianco stood six feet to my right, his hand lowered.

"Nothing ever against your will, my friend," he said, "but the offer stands."

Vale stamped up to him and slapped him, surprising him, connecting where I hadn't.

St. Bianco's face snapped sideways, then turned and glowered at her.

"Vale," he said.

"You bastard. All *you* ever offer is death. You're as much a part of this fucked-up world as any other rotting corpse. Just because your flesh doesn't stink, you think you're better?"

St. Bianco said nothing, only returned Vale's stare. Long seconds passed. The silence in the room developed an almost physical presence. Then the lobby darkened. It took me a moment to realize the glow of the holy folks had dimmed. St. Bianco returned to his chair and grew still, like the others, only their eyes betraying the faintest hint of animation. The gloom deepened. The holy folk faded into it. A sweet aroma like honey wafted into the air. I inched closer to the dead people and squinted, wondering if I saw what I thought I saw, wondering if wet, crimson tears really flowed from St. Bianco's eyes and down his withered cheeks.

ELEVEN

Erika and Octavio set us up with rooms on the fourth floor. No power, so we used the stairs.

The previous occupants had removed the electronic door locks. You could lock yourself in with the latch and the manual deadbolt, but you couldn't lock it from the other side. Not that stealing or any other crime posed much trouble, Octavio explained. We could take pretty much anything we needed or wanted from the shops in the city—and the dead holy folks had a way of weeding out bad apples upon arrival.

They housed us all in a row, our rooms overlooking the streetfront and the beach. Clean sheets, comfortable furniture, and working bathrooms. A little taste of heaven to go with the saints. Della and I roomed next to Christopher, with Birch on the other side. Then Vale, and then Gordon and Dawson, and part of me felt herded, livestock penned in stalls for the night. Except that night, the locals invited us to their party.

A bonfire roared on the beach. Flames licked twenty feet into the air, spitting embers into the dark. The smoke almost vanished against the night sky. Surf rolled onto the sand and brought a rhythmic pulse, the beat of an enormous hidden heart. The pulse of the Earth itself, carrying on, indifferent, while humanity died and ravened its own bones. A crowd gathered, a few hundred strong, with beach chairs and blankets spread round the blaze, and I thought if this was everyone in Miami, then the living stood little chance of outlasting the dead.

A group of musicians played music by the fire. Mellow, relaxing songs. Bob Marley. The Grateful Dead. The Beach Boys. Eternal beach music. People knew all the words and sang along. Some got up and danced. Della and I watched Christopher throw a glow-in-the-dark frisbee back and forth with some kids his age. Nearby sat Dawson and Gordon, snuggled together on a beach blanket, singing, almost happy. Beside them but alone sat Vale, back to the fire, gaze steady on the enormous blank canvas of the Atlantic Ocean and the starry night sky.

This defined our world now, this little pocket of safety with our backs pressed to the sea. Nowhere left to retreat. Our trust in a group of beings we would've called monsters in another life. Too stunned and numbed to feel much horror anymore. We could stay, enjoy a comfortable room, the beach, the community of the living, but like the other places I'd found myself since I lost Evelyn, it didn't belong to me. I was living in someone else's space, living by their rules, by their authority, enjoying security they provided, and that always came with a cost, an obligation. It required trust too, but my reserves of trust had long ago scraped bottom.

Lohatchie called to me the strongest when I found myself like this, with time to catch my breath. My place down there beckoned. Lohatchie would be mine, Della's, Christopher's, and Birch's if he wanted, and the only authority there would be our own.

A truck grumbled onto the sand from one of the wide, paved paths through the park.

The music faded out. Voices quieted.

An old municipal pick-up truck with fat tires for the beach, it rumbled along, towing a cargo trailer equipped with an iron mesh cage. Probably once used to house tools needed to clean and maintain the beach, it now held half a dozen wormfeeders banging around inside, jostled by the motion and their own attraction to the living.

It stopped by the bonfire. The crowd gave a riotous cheer. They clapped and whooped when the driver emerged and waved his baseball cap at them.

The frisbee game ended. Christopher dropped to his knees in the sand beside me.

"What's going on?" he said.

The fire glowed dull against dead flesh but glistened in the living eyes glaring out from it. It flickered on the faces of the living, filled with child-like anticipation. People encircled the truck with ritualistic excitement, and the band launched into that old song about not fearing the reaper. It transported me back to the prison yard, back to a warden with the faith of a martyr, who built gallows and a bonfire to separate sinners from saints and send us all to our just reward. The driver and others reached into the truck bed and dragged out long poles with wire loops at the end.

"Cornell?" Christopher said. "You all right?"

Della put her hand on mine.

"They're going to burn them," I said.

"Where'd they come from?" he said.

Octavio walked up to us then and gave the answer.

"These are stragglers from the city limits," he said. "They never make it far, but we clean them out just the same. Catch a few every day. Then we bring them here and remind them this is a place for the living. Makes everyone feel better to see them burn."

"Not everyone," I said.

"Why don't you join in? You're the newbs. They'll let you throw one on the fire."

Della's fingers tightened around my arm.

"Can we?" Christopher said.

He didn't understand the harsh face I showed him. "No, we'll pass."

"Suit yourself." Octavio moved on to speak with Dawson and Gordon, who took him up on the offer and walked over to the truck. Vale declined.

A group of four men and women looped wires around the neck of the first wormfeeder then used the poles to wrangle it off the trailer. It stumbled and fell in the sand. Laughter rippled from the crowd. The dead thing rose to its feet and swiped at them, gnashed its teeth. People threw trash and seashells at it, ran up, and jabbed it with sticks. A kid, maybe fifteen years old, rushed in and stuck a beach hat on its head. That brought guffaws.

The four working the poles spun the thing around, the poles like spokes on a wheel, the walking corpse its axle. One of the women tripped, fell, and let go of her pole. The wormfeeder raged at her, dragging the others with it until another woman seized the loose pole. Laughter again. As if a slapstick comedy routine played out in jest. This was sport to them. The first round ended when they shoved the wormfeeder into the fire then yanked the poles free, decapitating it with the wire. The other corpses rioted in the cage while the first one burned.

"Let's call it a night," Della said. "We don't need to watch this."

"Take Christopher and go ahead," I said. "I'll come along soon. Need to think some more, or I won't be able to sleep a damn minute."

"Don't be long."

"Nope."

Della ushered Christopher off the beach. The boy glanced back at the fire half a dozen times, confused, fascinated, frightened, trying to make sense of what he saw and how Della and I had reacted to it. Trying to understand the adult world when even the adults didn't understand it anymore. I laid back on the sand and listened to the waves break on the beach, wishing for them to drown out the voices around me.

Someone screamed. I sat up, startled, but the scream turned into laughter.

Over at the fire, Dawson and Gordon each held one of the long poles and grappled with the corpse of an obese woman in a tracksuit. Two others angled their loops over her head, and the four wrestled the wormfeeder toward the blaze.

Vale stepped in front of me, blocking my view. I hadn't heard her approach on the soft sand. "Let's talk," she said.

I couldn't read her face. Too many conflicting emotions—and a kind of hard-edged nerve I'd never seen before. I stood and brushed sand off me.

"What's on your mind?"

"This place." She led us toward the water. "Doesn't feel right, does it?"

"Every place has secrets."

"St. Bianco has secrets for sure."

"How do you know him?"

"He turned up at the airport up in Actsburg out of the blue one evening. Set everything on its head, tried to warn us an army of wormfeeders would overrun the place. Everything turned to shit, and I lost a lot of friends."

"Was he right about the wormfeeders?"

"Yeah. Only me, Dawson, Gordon, and Gallegos escaped. Wormfeeders got Gallegos a few weeks later. But she didn't rise, like we said. That's what St. Bianco offered us, a blessing to keep us dead when we died. Real death. He came to see us all die."

"You'd think with all the people we lose these days, it'd get easier, but it doesn't. Still hurts the same. We just don't have time for grieving."

"Maybe that's why I don't like this place. I don't want time to think."

"There's more to it than that, though. I don't like this place because it's a prison like the one I broke out of at the start of this nightmare."

"You were in prison?"

"I robbed banks. On my last job, a dumbass security guard shot and killed my girlfriend. She was pregnant. I killed him and two other guards, then let myself get caught and pled guilty. I wanted to be punished, not for killing the guards, though I regret that, but for failing Evelyn. She could handle herself, never really needed me to protect her or watch over her—except that one time, and I blew it."

"I used to want that, to be protected. That's some bullshit, though. You take care of yourself, because when things go bad—really, really bad like they are now—all the protectors worry about their own ass first. My boyfriend, my parents, they all abandoned me, left me on my own for weeks alone in my apartment before I worked up the nerve to go out. I don't like this place because it's a daydream. A little pocket of pretending life can go on the way it did before the dead started walking. I gave up living in daydreams the day I set foot outside my safe, little hole. I prefer the real world even when it's doing its damndest to kill me. At least I'm living on my own terms then."

She sounded so much like Evelyn, my heart ached for my old life.

We stopped shy of the surf line. Waves broke and pushed froth and foam within inches of our feet, then dragged it back into the sea. The faint light of the bonfire danced across Vale's face. For a moment, I saw Evelyn in her features, and my chest tightened.

"We do what we do, what we have to do. We go on living," she said. "I never want to depend on anyone else again. Not my parents, not my boyfriend, not swaggering assholes who think they're better than everyone else, and certainly not a dead saint. No one. It hurt me bad to find my freedom. Wounded me, scarred me. I healed stronger. I won't ever give that up again."

My head throbbed, and my eyes welled up.

Reality cracked. For several moments, a cloud of confusion enveloped me.

I plunged back in time to a night before a bank job, standing beside Evelyn, each of us reassuring the other, sharing our confidence, our fates inextricably entwined.

Vale took my hand and pulled me close. Her warmth reminded me of Evelyn, and, god, she seemed so much like her, a woman who'd protect *us* before she ever needed me to protect her, a woman who understood life only counted if you played by your own rules.

The firelight glinted in her eyes. I stared into them, speechless.

"Cornell? You okay?" she said.

She leaned closer to my face, worried, watching me. Her breath glided across my lips.

She took my other hand and eased herself closer to me, our legs touching.

I sensed her desire to kiss me. My body responded with yearning. Part of me wanted it to happen, wanted to yield to the moment—but the rest of me knew what I felt I felt for a ghost, for Evelyn and memories Vale stirred, but not for Vale.

Back in the hotel, Della and Christopher waited for me, and somewhere far down the road, Lohatchie, but on the beach, men and women burned the living dead, while the world died all around us, and this woman offered me a connection to emotions that had lain dormant since Evelyn died. Why, when the world was ending, should I hold myself back from anything good? Anything that meant *life* meant *living*?

A high wave broke and flooded our feet. Vale yelped.

We let go of each other's hands and rushed to dry sand. The ocean washed the temptation away and left me grateful for its intervention.

Vale offered me a long, uncertain, possibly hopeful gaze. I looked away, walked away, left her standing alone on the beach, regretting every step. She might be the most "alone" person I'd ever met. I wished I could give her the connection she sought, but some people, that's their fate, their role in life, the only way they can survive and be who they are.

I looked back once from the shadows of the sidewalk.

Vale stood with her back to me.

Barely visible in the firelight, a thin, pale woman against the dead, blank ocean.

TWELVE

Whatever misgivings I had about shacking up in the Most Holy South Beach Realm of the Living, I couldn't deny how much Della and Christopher enjoyed sunbathing on the beach and swimming in the ocean. No matter where our path led, the destination could wait a few days while they enjoyed the respite. Birch, on the other hand, never left his room. I brought him food and found him in the same position every time. Hunched over at the little desk, scribbling in his notebooks. Vale and I avoided each other. Della didn't hide that she sensed the energy between us, but she said nothing about it.

Dawson and Gordon fell right into the beach life. They made friends fast and became part of the community. I envied their happiness and satisfaction to a degree. I couldn't wrap my head around it, but people need different things in life. For some, removal of fear beats confronting and eliminating it. Like a dog hiding its head under a chair. They can't see you, they figure you can't see them. But the cause of those fears remains.

Motivated by curiosity, I dropped by the dead holy folk a few times a day and peeked in the window or sat in the cool gloom of the lobby. Nothing about them ever changed. They sat on makeshift thrones in utter stillness, unblinking eyes staring straight ahead as if they saw past the world into another beyond it, a realm outside ordinary senses, a vision world that revealed its secrets only to them.

I dreamt every night. The Red Man showed me the approaching darkness.

In my dreams, it flowed like vantablack acid devouring the substance of the universe.

I couldn't tell if something drove it, or if it moved of its own volition.

It consumed the light, the planets, stars, galaxies, and nebulas, which all appeared like backgrounds for cartoons set in space where everything looks crammed together and close as hell and spaceships zip from planet to planet. The dark spread like ink spilled across an animation cell. When it ate enough of whatever scene played in my mind, it burst alive with human eyes, all looking my way as if they saw into my soul.

I woke up sweating then, every night for all the few days we spent in Miami. But I told no one about the dreams. I think Birch knew, though. From the way he looked when I brought him meals, I think similar visions invaded his sleep.

Those dreams wore me down.

Out on the road, with the dead everywhere, staying alive distracted me. I could wake up, shrug them off, and ignore them again until nightfall. Staying alive, keeping Christopher, Della, and Birch alive, held them at bay. But not here. Walking down pretty sidewalks, sitting on the beach, lounging in palm tree shade did not take them away. When I looked at waves breaking and crashing, the tide ebbing and flowing, the dreams rippled alongside. Sometimes I swam with Christopher and became lost in thought, afloat on the edge of an ocean that could swallow me in a moment. I walked the beach with Della, and the rhythm of the surf, the heartbeat of the earth slowed, wound down toward its last pump of blood to the body on which we lived.

Surrounded by beauty and peace, warmth and light, by people who smiled and didn't take every step, every breath in fear it might be their last, I sensed the world dying.

I lost track of how many times Della asked me what was on my mind.

How could I explain? To describe my dreams made them sound childish. I knew no words to convey the sense of abject nothingness, of despair, of anger that burned with more power and fury than the heart of a star in that vast darkness.

She let me be when I refused to answer. Let me work it out for myself.

My saddest point came the moment I did exactly that.

More than the dreams themselves, more than the dark horror they predicted, what left me most unsettled and fearful was that Miami provided a true taste of our future. We could run to Lohatchie, sure, and we stood a good chance of making it safe and sound given how good we'd become at navigating this world of the dead. We could escape the wormfeeders and the living alike. Make a home. But the dreams would come with me. That darkness would arrive one day. Until then, I'd live with it, every night, every morning. It would inhabit my mind. Rob me of the peace I sought. Once we hit Lohatchie, once we put the day-to-day struggle to survive behind us, I'd have all the time in the world to think about what was coming, to live life with that dream-imprinted horror, under the shadow of the Red Man, and, goddamn him, I understood then that what he'd done to me made it impossible for me to turn away.

I couldn't break out of this prison like I'd escaped Warden Grove.

I couldn't drive away down the broken highway the way we'd left behind Camp Cady and Deadtown.

The Red Man had latched onto my soul, a metaphysical tick bloating himself off my peace of mind. His burden would travel with me everywhere for as long as I lived or until the darkness snuffed us all out of existence.

Even if that happened tomorrow, it would be too long for me.

The morning I reached that conclusion, it came while Della and I sat high on a lifeguard's chair to watch the sunrise. In the growing dawn, she fell asleep with her head on my shoulder.

She sensed the change in me, the tension of confusion that left my body, the new tension of determination that replaced it. She woke and kissed me.

"There's something I've got to do, Della," I said. "And I'm sorry. So, so sorry."

She studied my face then kissed me again.

"I know," she said as if she had all along and only waited for me to catch up. "Promise me one thing?"

"What's that?"

"Wherever you have to go, whatever you do, do it for yourself, for *us*, not for *them*."

"Yeah, I promise you that. Everything I do now, I do for us. Always."

She kissed me once more. We embraced until the sun floated free over the horizon.

I dropped down from the chair, crossed the sand, walked to the lobby where the dead holy folk sat in motionless contemplation. They seemed different now, more substantial, more real. More credible. The calming effect of their proximity irked me. I walked to the lobby bar and plucked a straw from a bin there. I tore off one end of the paper and slid the remainder halfway off the straw. Standing before St. Bianco, I raised the straw to my lips and blew. The paper shot like a spear, struck his wrinkled nose, and bounced away.

After a few seconds, his eyes lowered to meet my gaze.

"All right, you crazy dead saint, let's talk about how we kill the Red Man."

THIRTEEN

How do you kill what's already dead?

The dead holy folks provided no straight answer.

Instead, they demanded I spend days fasting and meditating to prepare myself and my soul for the confrontation to come. I laughed at the idea, picturing myself sitting my ass on the beach and humming "Ommmm" for hours at a time while pondering the secrets of the universe, but they didn't mean that. Meditation doesn't begin to describe what they did to me.

After giving me time to say goodbye to Della and Christopher, they locked me in with them in part of the hotel basement. No food, only water. No light except for a single, battery-powered lantern.

In that milky darkness, the dead holy folks took turns putting me through an experience I'd only had once before, back in Deadtown—when the Red Man transported me into a vision of his past to show me how Darrell Philip Stradley had transformed from a convenience-store stock clerk to a death-cult leader to a master of the living dead. Stradley had touched me and sent me on a wild ride of visions. As each of the dead holy folks did the same, I learned they all shared a similar path. Each, like Stradley, heard a calling. Some believed it came from God, others from the universe, or the spirit world, or Nirvana, or some other deity, force, or entity I'd never heard of, and even one made up by a woman who'd believed in nothing at all before it spoke to her. She called it Princess, after her childhood cat.

One by one, they brought me into their heads. The dark basement faded away and filled with their histories. I lived the memories of their first contact with the spark that launched them to sainthood, priesthood, shamanhood, whateverhood...

A vision in a dream.

A voice from the oldest tree in the woods.

A fire in the sky only she could see.

A sense of infinite peace that shaped his every choice.

A fox and a deer in the wild.

The drumming of the surf upon the shore.

I heard each call the same as them, felt its compulsion in my bones, and saw the hope they'd found in it. Religion and its trappings never held much stock for me. If I didn't care for society's basic rules of the road, why would I want to bow to some invisible authority whose existence I had to believe in for it to matter? I understood its appeal, though. After sharing their experiences, I couldn't deny the substance of it—except as it turned out, I was right too, at least partly.

I'd relived St. Bianco's struggle with his inner darkness, the miracles that demonstrated its defeat. He beat the dark side of himself into submission, cast his entire being toward the light, worked wonders in our world—and what became of him when he died? What did he find waiting for him out in the grand hereafter?

The same damn thing as Darrell Philip Stradley, madman and vicious killer, and all the dead souls who'd returned to earth: not a goddamn thing.

Absence.

Void.

No heaven or hell. No reward, no punishment.

No return to life reincarnated in a higher or lower form.

No greater understanding of the path to Nirvana.

No unification with the fabric of reality.

No ultimate purpose designed by the Universe.

No community of spirits.

Not even the peace of their raw energy recycled by the cosmos, their lifeforce scattered to the stars and interstellar dust.

They found only themselves and the countless souls of others set adrift in the same utter blankness, where only the voice of Darrell Philip Stradley offered anything to cling to and orient themselves. Darrell Philip Stradley, who in life led a cult with the motto, "Death of the flesh to free the spirit, death of the spirit to free the flesh." Stradley, who'd killed, maimed, and tortured dozens, many with their consent and encouragement. Stradley, who'd built an arsenal and bought nerve gas on the black market to spread his gospel of death. Stradley, who'd died from a bullet to the heart fired by Birch. In the nothing that followed life, his voice ruled. His will rallied the souls of the dead for their assault on the living.

What did the dead holy folk do?

They watched.

Unlike ordinary souls, theirs remained tethered to their incorruptible corpses, and their faith led them to passivity. If utter emptiness followed life, it meant they hadn't fully grasped the purpose of the divine. They accepted it. The darkness flowed right in without any one of them lifting a finger to stop it. Thus Stradley rose again and became the Red Man, one of the guides and masters of the dead and the darkness. One of several around the world.

Whatever divinity existed in the universe, it looked and behaved nothing like what all the priests and prophets said. A damn big part of it boiled with... I don't know, hate? Evil? Words failed to equal the hostility and the craving for annihilation that lived in that darkness on its way to finish what the living dead had started.

Life and light repulsed it.

Warmth infuriated it.

Joy devoured its metaphysical guts like a violent cancer.

It sought to eliminate those things to preserve itself. Where was the light to balance the dark in all this? Somewhere in the vastness of existence, the dead holy folk assured me, light still existed, still shone on some far corner of reality, but not ours anymore. Not on humanity. Not on our very, very lost souls. The universe turns. Balances shift. Day follows night on a cosmic scale incomprehensible to me. And trust me, those dead freaks tried to make me understand, to show me what they knew. Every one of them.

I couldn't, though, not like them.

My brain could only wrap itself around the surface of their lessons. I couldn't explain or articulate it even to myself. The knowledge simply existed inside me, ready to guide me. All of this I saw and experienced, the memories of days, weeks, months, even years that unfolded around me in the span of seconds.

I watched souls leave their bodies and travel into the blackness.

I listened to ghostly screams of horror and despair.

Only their eyes remained vivid when they passed to the next world. Everything else about them turned amorphous and hazy.

Each dead holy person shared their death with me, and I died with them, over and again, witnessing their transcendence and the iridescent, ethereal tether that linked their soul to their corpse. The only lights in the void. A brightness other souls shunned because it reminded them that they hadn't lived a good enough life to escape the darkness. They clustered instead around the deep, red glow of Stradley's tether, moths to a terrible flame. When Stradley opened the way for their return, that light guided them into dead flesh.

The seventh and final dead holy person to share her memories with me reminded me of Della. A nurse, she'd died from a disease that infected her while she worked overseas to save the lives of children during a hemorrhagic fever outbreak. No coincidence, the healer went last. The experiences so far wore me down to a raw nerve, too tired to even sip water. The only saving grace came in escape from the dreams with which the Red Man afflicted me. After the last holy woman showed me her story, she embraced me, and her touch, her energy restored me.

I slept then on the floor of the basement.

Hours or days later, I woke alone and made my way to the hotel lobby.

The dead holy folks sat in their chairs, stony and impassive.

My whole body trembled with hunger.

Octavio came and helped me to a chair. Erika brought me food.

Minutes later, Della came, summoned by Ruth. She sat and held my hand while I ate, and my strength returned.

"How long was I down there?" I asked as Erika refilled my water glass.

"A week," Della said. "What did they do to you?"

"Showed me things."

Erika dragged over a chair and sat across from me. "What did you see? They know so much but tell us so little."

I tried to answer. I wanted to answer. I had no words to describe the vastness of the knowledge and experience they'd conveyed.

When I finished eating, Erika cleared away the plates and utensils. Octavio helped me up, but I needed less assistance now. I felt almost myself again, at least physically.

St. Bianco stood from his chair.

The lobby brightened. A honey-sweet aroma perfumed the air.

Crimson tears ran from St. Bianco's eyes, down his cheek, and soaked into his clothes.

The other holy folk bled too. Some from their noses or ears, some from their hands, some from their lips, from their gums. One bled from a hole in his throat. Permutations of stigmata.

An atmosphere of tranquility settled upon us. All fear and sadness evaporated. Joy and relief did not replace it. Only a sense of rightness remained, as if no matter what came next, all would soon be okay. Even Della relaxed against me, tension and worry drained from her body.

Yet, I still resisted.

In the back of my mind, red flags waved, and warning sirens blared, buried deep but still there. As St. Bianco tilted his head to speak, a hot breath of bad air tickled my neck, reminding me no matter how things seemed, that my jackal waited, always on the fringes of my life, ready to chow down on my corpse when death finally took me.

"You're as prepared as we can make you, Mr. Cornell," St. Bianco said. "I'd hoped to impart you with a better understanding, a deeper appreciation for the divine within us all, but your mind and soul resisted with great determination."

"I'm stubborn like that," I said.

"Indeed, you are. We grant you a day of rest. You shall leave tomorrow morning."

As I nodded agreement, Della dug her fingers into my hand.

The dead holy folks dismissed us, and then she led me to the beach.

"You're going to face the Red Man," she said.

"That's the plan."

"I don't want you to go. Let's leave tonight. You, me, Christopher, and Birch. We'll blow out of here for Lohatchie."

"Tried that already. The Red Man won't let go of me and Birch."

"Fuck this life. Someone's always got their claws in you, digging for a pound of flesh."

"That's why I robbed banks. Turn the tables on things."

"How'd that work out for you?"

I laughed, not a shred of humor in it.

"I'll go with you," Della said.

"What about Christopher?"

"He'll be safe here. He's already made so many friends. Dawson and Gordon will take care of him, I'm sure."

"Della, I don't know if..." About to say what an awful idea it would be for her to come with me, how much danger she'd face, it hit me hard how much I wanted her at my side and how often we'd saved each other's hide, and I said, "I don't know if I can do this without you."

Laughter trickled through the air then.

Not the kind that drifts up from people having fun on the beach.

The kind only I heard.

Jackal's laughter.

FOURTEEN

Next morning, Della and I packed our gear for the trip north.

We squared things with Christopher. He didn't like it, wanted to come with us, but one of his friends, a pretty, blue-eyed girl a year older than him, promised a beach picnic and eased the sting of staying behind.

We'd take the Camry, Della and I alone on the road again, uncertain of anything except our trust in each other and the need to buy our freedom at any cost.

Imagine my surprise when we stepped into the parking lot and found Octavio and Denny leaning against the hood of the Camry with AR-15s in hand. Birch stood with them, his hair a wild electric tangle in the morning sun, his wiry body back in those dirty old pants and the bright Hawaiian shirt, his traveling clothes. He kept one arm around Christopher, a protective gesture that raised every hair on the back of my neck. Our car sat parked beside Vale's truck, and Vale stood at the open back doors of the rot-mobile. Time did nothing to improve its odor. The sight that set my heart racing, though, was St. Bianco, poised between me, Della, and everyone else, left hand raised, palm outward, as if to bless us, his right hand hidden away inside his threadbare black sports jacket. He radiated no sense of calm now.

"What's all this?" I said. "You all here to wish us well?"

"In a sense, Mr. Cornell," St. Bianco said. "We're here to clarify matters for you."

"You spent a week inside my head doing that. If I don't see clearly enough by now, not much's going to change that."

"This matter is of a more worldly nature. You'll easily understand," he said.

Octavio stepped forward. "Something you need to get through your thick skull."

"What's that?" I said.

"The dead holy folks, Cornell, put fuck-all stock in material things, including existence. All this here in Miami? This was always only temporary, waiting for you and the others like you who never showed. Now they've done what they needed to here. No one else is coming. They're ready to move on."

"Okay, so? Who's stopping them?"

"Us," Denny said.

"If you destroy the Red Man, there's a chance for life to survive in this part of the world. If you fail, it falls to the dead," Octavio said. "We fall to the dead."

"High stakes, I know," I said.

"The Red Man placed his mark on you for a reason." St. Bianco lowered his hand. "He sees potential in you, as do we, potential for you to sway the balance toward the light or the dark because of your refusal to live as others demand. If you fall to him and fail to return here, we'll have to assume you tilted toward death."

"If that happens, they won't let the dead have us," Octavio said.

Into the uncomfortable silence that followed, an upbeat, happy pop song from someone's boombox on the strip intruded, all high-pitched voices and jangly percussion.

"If things go the dead's way, Cornell," Vale said, "the holy folks will bless everyone here like St. Bianco did for my people in Actsburg, then send them to the next life before leaving."

"You mean they'll kill them," I said.

"It will be a blessing for them, Mr. Cornell," St. Bianco said. "We won't abandon them to the world to come if you fail."

"We prefer to live either way," Octavio said. "So, to give you an incentive not to fuck up and to make it back here, we're keeping Della."

"No fucking way," I said. "Della goes with me. Christopher too. I won't leave them here if you're thinking this crazy."

Octavio raised his AR-15, aimed it at my face. "Not a discussion, Cornell."

Denny approached with his rifle ready, seized Della by the arm, then dragged her aside. "We're not making you go alone, though."

I looked at Vale. "You?"

"Yeah," she said. "And Birch. St. Bianco insisted."

"He, too, bears the Red Man's mark. He, too, has a part to play," St. Bianco said.

"Just like that, you take my people hostage and expect me to do you a favor? After all I've endured on your behalf?"

"Have you forgotten so much already, Mr. Cornell?" St. Bianco said. "You're helping all of living humanity, how little of it remains. A favor not to us but to the light that burns low in the universe now. There's so much more at risk than we were able to convey to you. If you saw as we do, you'd know this is the right way, that your individuality, your wants and desires, your *people* mean nothing compared to the endless struggle that defines universal existence."

"You son of a bitch," I said. "It always comes down to this, doesn't it? Saint, sinner, or butt-headed fuck-up, you never give a rat's ass for anyone else's life. You grind us down under your authority simply because you fucking *can* and destroy everything anyone under you tries to build. Do you do it because you're afraid we might challenge you, maybe surpass you? Or do you do it simply because you have the power? Or because we don't give a rat's ass what you think, and you can't bear to be ignored?"

Octavio nudged Birch with his rifle. Birch moved and picked up the bags and gear Della and I had brought. He threw it in the back of Vale's truck then climbed in after it. Vale shut the doors.

"You're wasting daylight, asshole," Denny said.

Della spit on him. The saliva slapped his cheek.

He let go of her and recoiled, swiping the moisture away. Della snatched the gun from his hands before he knew he'd lost it. When he realized it, he froze, eye-to-eye with the barrel of his own weapon. Octavio switched his aim from me to Della.

"Careful now, Della," I said.

"Give that back to Denny, or I'll shoot you," Octavio said.

I drew my Beretta, aimed at Octavio. "Not if I shoot you first, jackass."

The tension linked us all, and that damn pop song kept crashing along, all cymbals and a high-pitched refrain, so insufferably fucking mirthful, but none of it mattered because St.

Bianco, who I hadn't even seen move, now held Christopher by the shoulders, the fingers of his left hand spread across his throat, his other still tucked away out of sight.

"Mr. Cornell," he said. "If you wish to back out of our plans, we can simply give all the people here our final blessing today and move on to our next endeavor."

Della's eyes widened at the sight of Christopher, who'd paled, his eyes glassy with fear. She lowered the gun, handed it back to Denny. I put mine away. Octavio lowered his.

"Some kind of saint you are," I said.

Octavio glared at me. "Don't think any of *us* wanted this. Now, go."

I locked gazes with Della, and we reached a silent agreement. She nodded.

"I'll be back for you, I promise. For you and Christopher," I said, then switched on the voice I'd relied on to scare the shit out of bank employees and patrons, security guards, and even cops and FBI agents during my long-lost life of crime: "I come back and find either one of them hurt, mistreated, or worse, you'll learn exactly how much I understand about the true nature of life and death."

FIFTEEN

We drove almost an hour before we saw more than one or two of the dead at a time.

My skin bristled at the change in the air when we exceeded the last reaches of the dead holy folk's protective energy and rolled out exposed. Traveling in Vale's wide, bulky truck proved more difficult than the smaller Camry, which Della knew well how to steer through tight passages among ruined cars and other debris. Several times Birch and I hopped out to clear the road, once even to shove aside what looked like an entire household-worth of second-hand furniture spilled from an overpacked pick-up truck flipped onto its side.

None of us spoke more than necessary. Vale drove, eyes steady on the road. Birch scribbled in yet another damn notebook. I wondered what he wrote, but I feared the answer. Kept thinking of the scene in that old movie about the caretaker trying to write a novel in a haunted hotel, but only typing the same phrase, again and again, *ad infinitum.*

So, mostly, I stared out the window and counted the dead.

We passed a group of five, the largest yet. Their bodies swiveled to track our progress. Eyes opened on every bit of their flesh. Watching us.

The Red Man knew we were on our way.

What that meant, I don't know. Neither did I know what the dead holy folks intended for us to do to him. For all the knowledge they'd drilled into my head, they never said how to kill the Red Man for good. I'd have to figure it out for myself as if required by some cosmic rules of the game, as if it wouldn't count if someone slipped me the answer. Fine. Robbing banks fair and square was one thing, but I had never been a cheater.

Somewhere north of Fort Lauderdale, we rolled up on a roadblock, a line of delivery vans stretched across the road. A woman with a guitar sat in a lawn chair in front of it. She wore a tie-died tank top with a peace sign printed on it, a pair of denim cutoffs, and no shoes. A hand-scrawled sign beside her read *"Michele Kutner, Acoustic Stylings and Folk Ramblings, CDs $15."* Below the sign, an open suitcase held an untidy pile of CD cases. The cover art featured a photo of a hawk.

Vale stopped the truck.

The woman strummed, not even lifting her eyes to notice us. Matted, blonde hair hooded her face.

"That's a new one," I said. "Footloose and fancy-free."

"What's she doing?" Vale said.

"Free concert. You want to go throw money in her hat and ask her to play 'Freebird,' or should we turn this hunk of junk around and find another way forward?"

"Turn around?"

"Yep, that's my vote too. We got enough of our own troubles. Don't need whatever she's got to offer added to the list."

Vale put the truck in reverse, started to back it up, but then hit the brake as she looked in the oversized side-view mirror.

"Shit. Looks like the rest of the band showed up," she said.

Movement in the passenger-side mirror revealed a group of men approaching. They wore long-sleeve shirts, jeans, even jackets despite the heat and humidity, with caps pulled down over their eyes and mirrored shades. In their hands, baseball bats, rifles, and knives.

"Must be a death-metal group," I said.

Vale glared at me, surprised, then laughed.

"Run them over," I said.

She shook her head. "They attack the tires, give us a couple of flats, we're cooked."

I cracked the window. Guitar music drifted in, something lazy and mellow I didn't recognize. Low voices came with it.

"Sounds like a lot of them out there."

Vale lifted her rifle from where she'd stashed it alongside her seat. "I'll go up on top of the truck and give you cover. You get out and convince them to leave us alone."

"You make it sound easy."

"Trust me. Not one of them will get near you, and if they try, I'll send them running."

"Not a great plan. There's way more of them than us. If we stay here too long, we'll lose any chance at all to get away, but, okay, let's try it your way. I've bluffed my way out of worse odds."

I checked my Beretta and then stepped out of the truck.

The guitar music ended. The approaching men stopped. The driver's side door clicked open. Bumping and thumping told me Vale had gone up top. Guitar girl looked up from her instrument. Her hair parted from her face, revealing skin so pale it almost reached translucence and dark rings around her eyes. She appeared quite ill. A dead eater.

"Shit," I muttered.

One of the men threw a rock at me. It missed and pinged off the side of the truck.

"Hey! Don't look at her. You look at me," he said. "Over here. Look at me."

I did. "Go easy there, chief, I'm just an avid Michele Kutner fan. It's a treat to hear her play live. Or sort of live, I guess."

The man pushed his cap back on his head and revealed his own pallid, deathly face.

"Hey, Vale," I said. "Pretty sure they're hoping to make us dinner. *Their* dinner, I mean."

She didn't speak, only thumped the truck twice in reply.

"Go ahead and put that gun down, mister," the rock-thrower said.

"Nope," I said. "Listen up, we're going to turn around, go back the way we came, and you're going to let us go. I promise you don't want to mess with us."

"That so? You got an army hiding in there? Way I see it, there's twenty of us and two of you. I ain't no bookie, but those seem like good odds to me."

"Take my word, they're not. You don't know who you're dealing with."

"Oh, yeah? Who are we dealing with?"

I didn't know the answer. Me and Birch, sure, on our own we'd be screwed, going down with a fight. What had Vale meant to trust her? What did she intend to do? I leaned hard into the tone of voice that had sent bank patrons and workers face down on the floor and kept them there, while Evelyn and I collected loot. The tone of voice that ignited primal, animal fear in the base of their spines.

"You want to know you can find out the hard way. Or you can back off and let us leave."

The man hesitated, so slight someone else might've missed it. But I knew that pause. It meant uncertainty. "Can't do it, no way, no how. We're too damn hungry."

He gestured. The man at his left pressed the stock of his rifle to his shoulder and aimed at me. A gunshot cracked the air. Blood spurted from the rifleman's throat. He staggered backward, dropped his weapon, then fell over, dead. Three others with guns lifted them. More gunshots, one atop the other, rolling thunder that echoed along the road. Each gunman took a bullet in the same place, through the throat, out the back of the neck, then fell. A shot that severed the spinal cord and left the reanimated corpse paralyzed. What an incredible shot to make, and not one missed. It happened so fast my brain lagged at puzzling out that Vale was doing the shooting. The gunmen down, she turned to those with blades. Men dropped like wasps falling from a nest sprayed with pesticide. Rock-thrower hunched with an arm over his head, hopped this way and that to dodge the carnage. Bullets ripped into the knees of those carrying bats and other weapons, crippling them, and then only the rock-thrower and the guitar woman remained unscathed. All this in the span of seconds.

When the reverberations of Vale's last shot died, I approached the rock-thrower where he crouched with his arms covering his face and head.

"You found out the hard way," I said.

Trembling, he looked up at me, into my silhouette with the sun at my back.

"Who the fuck are you?" he said.

"We're the people you should've let go in peace, dumbass."

I braced my foot against one of his shoulders and pushed him down. He fell without any resistance and curled into a defenseless ball. I kicked him in the side to keep him there.

The truck clanked. Vale clambered down from the roof, smoke wisping from the barrel of her rifle. She grinned at me as she slung it from her shoulder.

I squinted at her. "Trust you, you said."

"Aren't you glad you did?"

"How the hell did you learn to shoot like that?"

Vale grinned, shrugged. "Just came naturally first time I picked up a rifle."

"Bullshit."

"True story, swear to God."

Vale crossed her heart, a childhood gesture, and laughed, and almost started me laughing too, but then the men Vale had killed began to reanimate. None of them could move with their spines severed, but they sure could grunt and moan. I wanted nothing more than to leave this ugly patch of road and continue our mission, but the road wasn't done with us. A scream burst into the air. In the corner of my eye, a flash of swirled colors and tangled, blonde hair signaled to me that Michele still contained plenty of fight. She swung a machete at my head. I dropped fast. The blade swished over me and clanked against the truck.

She raised it over her head for another blow, but I lunged before she could swing.

My right shoulder pounded into her abdomen as I lifted her from the ground and smashed her against the truck's armored fender. She growled in my ear.

The machete slashed wildly, missing my back, but soon enough, she'd hit me.

I'd lost track of Michele after the shooting started. She must have hidden until things calmed down. It made no sense for her to attack now. She should've run off and taken cover until we left. Hunger made people stupid, and Vale had called it: The dead-eaters weren't right in the head.

The machete scraped my lower back. I struggled to shift my weight and push the woman to the ground, but she tangled herself with me, tying up my limbs. The blade nicked my ass. She growled in my ear; a gunshot obliterated the sound as her head exploded in my face. Blood and gore showered me. All the tightness evacuated her body. Concert over, no encore. I staggered under her dead weight, then slid myself free and let her corpse flop to the ground, the machete still clutched in her hand.

After several stuttering steps, I dropped and sat on the road.

Vale's shadow fell over me. "You all right?"

"You could've hit *me* with that shot," I said.

"Only if I wanted to."

She offered me a hand, and I took it and pulled myself back on my feet.

Now I saw her through a wet, red haze covering my face. It seemed right, like staring at the angel of death, and I wondered what had made Vale who she was. She opened the back of the truck then returned to me with a towel. I wiped myself clean. Birch climbed out, looked around at the newly living dead, at the wounded crawling or dragging themselves to the roadsides. He looked me up and down, shook his head, then went back in.

I plucked a stone from the ground and hurled it at the rock-thrower. It struck his shoulder. He yelped and whimpered. I climbed back into the truck. Vale put it in gear and turned us around. Birch poked through the window from the back.

"Don't let us bother you, Birch. We're just keeping your ass alive," I said.

He nodded, then returned to his damn notebook.

The truck crunched over a body as we left the roadblock. I winced. Vale rolled her eyes.

The wheels sped up, and we returned to motion. The going only got tougher. The dead grew in number, the roads more clogged and difficult to pass. We drove north until dusk, then found a house to pass the night. The residents had boarded it up nice and tight as if preparing for a hurricane, and our truck squeezed into the attached two-car garage.

We heated canned soup in the fireplace and ate before taking turns standing watch.

Sometime after midnight, Vale woke me in the bed I'd taken on the second floor, rousing me from the first clean sleep I'd had in weeks. No dreams, not even my own.

"My watch already?" I said.

"No. You've got a couple of hours left, but you need to see this."

I clambered from bed and followed her to the master bedroom, where Birch sat on the edge of a king-size bed pointing at sliding glass doors that opened onto a small deck. I stepped out with Vale. The view overlooked a golf course, a manmade pond, and rows of houses like the one we occupied. Moonlight shone down, bright, austere, lighting the world like an old black-and-white movie. It took me time to process the view. The scale of it overwhelmed me. In the yard below, in the road, in the yards across the street, on the next block, as far as my eyes could see, the dead filled the world. Hundreds, more likely thousands. Wormfeeders in all states of decay and ruin, all facing our house—and all their eyes stared up at us, so many eyes opened in dead flesh, all turned to see the same thing at the same time, so many I imagined I heard them shifting wetly in unison, so many it looked as if the night sky with its stars and constellations had fallen to earth.

My stomach lurched. Sweat beaded on my forehead.

Vale used one of the deck chairs to boost herself onto the roof.

"Come up here," she said.

I did. From the roof peak, I saw the sight repeated on all sides of the house.

From every direction, the dead watched over us.

"The Red Man knows we're coming," I said.

"Oh, you think?" Vale said.

"This is why he didn't touch my dreams," I said. "He sent his nightmares in person."

"Why aren't they attacking?"

"Why would they? They're the welcoming committee."

SIXTEEN

By morning, the dead drifted off to wherever walking corpses go after dawn.

I had no idea how they came and went so quickly. I asked Birch what he thought, but he only scribbled a few words for me in his notebook: "The dead travel fast." I had told Christopher the same thing, and I glared at Birch, feeling like a patronized child. He shrugged. I knew the quote well, from *Dracula*, and it made me wish for a world where the monsters played by rules the way vampires did and the living outnumbered the dead. Such luxury!

We loaded into the truck then rolled out.

Here and there, a corpse watched us, its many eyes tracing our movements.

Vale drove slow, afraid of an ambush, but I knew none would come. The Red Man gained nothing from killing us. If I understood what the dead holy folks had shown me, he benefitted only if he turned us to his cause, to the service of the darkness.

A few miles down the road, a pattern emerged among the wormfeeders. The crowd from last night hadn't, in fact, wandered off so much as it had dispersed and now kept tabs on us. As we passed out of sight of one dead sentinel, another appeared.

The Red Man watched us through the eyes of the dead.

We traveled through his territory now, the territory of the dead, of the darkness.

Vale tensed, and her knuckles paled harsh white where she gripped the steering wheel.

"You and Della," she said, the first words spoken for almost an hour.

"What about us?" I said.

"I don't see it, don't see you two as a couple, I mean."

"Oh? You some kind of relationship expert?"

Vale laughed, much harder and longer than made sense to me.

"When the dead overran my town, I spent weeks alone in my apartment, worrying about my boyfriend trapped in his place on the other side of town," she said. "Eventually, when I left because I would've died if I didn't, I went to him. Guess what I found at his place?"

"I don't like guessing games."

"Fine. I found he'd been shacked up with another woman and gaslighting me the whole damn time. The one person I wanted to be with when the world ended wanted to be with another woman and lied to me about it. So, relationship expert? Not hardly."

"Sorry about that. He sounds like a world-class asshole."

"He was. That was another life. In the here-and-now, I see them with different eyes. I've lost everyone close to me. I'm more alone now than I was trapped by myself in my apartment, but I'm also, I don't know, happier, I guess, but that's not the right word. I'm not happy to live in this fucked-up world of the dead. But I know who I am better than ever before, and I know what I want and what I'm good at. I'd never have discovered my talent for shooting if the dead hadn't risen. Funny, right? Most people lost everything they had when the dead plague started. I gained everything I didn't have. I read people better than ever, and you and Della, I just don't see it."

"You think me and you make a better match?"

"Didn't say that. That's not what I'm saying."

"What are you saying?"

"That I... that I... well, I don't know what I'm saying. I don't see it. That's all."

"Duly noted, Miss Lonelyhearts."

"Whatever," Vale said.

The truck grumbled on along the road. The dead sentries doubled, came closer together, in pairs or trios now, all of them simply watching. I felt prison vibes, under constant scrutiny, laboring under the illusion of tiny liberties. We were all prisoners of some kind. Prisoners of the flesh, or our desires, or our blind spots, or destiny, or a world unrecognizable as our own. Even if we succeeded in killing the Red Man and the darkness never came, nothing much would change as long as the dead walked and things like St. Bianco and the dead holy folks existed. As long as people accumulated power and created authority to enforce their will on others, we remained imprisoned.

The sentinel groups numbered four, six, even ten in some clusters now.

"Getting closer," I said.

Half a mile later, we hit a four-way intersection, where the wormfeeder crowd stretched farther than the eye could see in all directions except west. Imagine the biggest concert or rally ever, an ocean of bodies, a sea of faces, painted gold by the sinking sun, but absolutely still and lifeless, except for the hard stare of innumerable eyes watching from wasting flesh.

Vale stopped the truck. "I've never seen so many of them," she whispered.

"I have," I said.

Deadtown streets filled with the dead in their masses. Here, though, even more gathered, maybe the entire southeast dead population. It took seven dead holy folks to create a bubble of life around Miami. It took the power of one, the Red Man, to fill an entire region with rot and death. The balance said a lot about our chances.

"If they attack, we're dead," Vale said. "Nowhere to run, and we can't fight them all."

"They're here to guide us. They left only one road open, heading west."

"It's a trap," Vale said.

"It always has been. We've been trapped since the dead rose."

A sad expression shaded Vale's face. "I was trapped long before that."

I didn't know what she meant, but it occurred to me I had been too. Trapped, physically, in prison, yeah, but, more importantly, trapped by my guilt for letting Evelyn die, for losing the future we planned together, for falling under the angry heel of the society I'd lived my whole life flipping off. Even afterward, trapped by circumstance, by dead people who pulled my puppet strings, trapped by my obligation to Della. That last notion hurt. I didn't want to think of Della that way. I *didn't* think of her that way. Vale had gotten under my skin. The way she'd talked about Della and me sounded an awful lot like what I imagine Evelyn would've said about us. I stopped myself from looking at Vale. Her face reminded me too much of Evelyn. I watched the dead. I shoved uncertainty from my mind.

"Good. We're on the same page. Keep driving," I said.

Vale shifted in her seat. I sensed her glaring at me but ignored her. I preferred to focus on the horror of a million walking corpses with eyes in every part of their flesh than look her in the eye and risk the cascade of old emotions she might instigate. I don't think I've ever heard the jackal laugh so loud and so hard in the entire time he'd stalked me.

"Well, fucking fine," Vale said.

She put the truck in gear and stamped on the gas. It lurched forward, and then she turned west. The dead didn't move as we passed them. Only their eyes did. The eyes of lost souls.

Clearer roads waited ahead, all of them lined by wormfeeders.

We made a one-truck parade for them to silently cheer. The odor of death permeated the air. It coated our nostrils, made our eyes water. Birch propped himself behind us, taking in the sight. We could've driven faster, but it seemed fitting to go slow, unhurried, as if unafraid, to let those greedy, malevolent eyes stare at the life they envied. A show of bravado, sure, but none of us were eager to reach the end of our journey. The route the dead allowed us led onto a highway. They blocked every exit, but one.

The road sign put a name to our destination.

Acme Wonderland.

The Red Man wanted to meet us on the site of one of my very few happy childhood memories. He wanted to confront us in a cartoon reality. I should have known.

I laughed hard.

Whether out of surprise or fear, I couldn't say.

SEVENTEEN

The entrance to Acme Wonderland loomed in the afternoon haze.

Wormfeeders streamed into the road behind us, cutting off our only escape route.

The theme park gates rose from either side of the road and formed an arch over the passage, once vibrant with color, now faded from neglect, painted with the most popular characters in the Acme Storyverse. Captain Capybara. Connie Caribou. Darlene Deer. Foxy Pinewood. Marvelous Moose. Polly Platypus. Clusters of decapitated heads hung down on wires and ropes from the top of the sign and covered the cheery cartoon faces, giving all the characters dead heads. A lazy rain of blood and putrescence drizzled onto the gates as the bodiless noggins squirmed and worked their useless jaws. A single lane stood open. Rows of Acme character costume heads—those big fuzzy ones actors wear to greet visitors—mounted on pikes funneled us toward it. The costume faces buzzed with flies dining on the stale blood and viscera smeared into the fabric and fur.

Vale drove us to the edge of the gate and stopped.

"I need a minute," she said. "Once we enter, we only leave if we kill the Red Man."

"We crossed that line quite a while ago," I said.

Birch placed a hand on my shoulder. I swiveled to see him. His expression confused me. Resignation and relief. Eagerness. The most relaxed I'd seen him since we met. Then it hit me how whatever came next would answer all the questions he'd hammered at since the dead plague began and free him of its mystery.

"The end is, indeed, fucking nigh," I said.

Birch smiled, his face full of deep wrinkles.

Vale drove through the gate.

Wormfeeders awaited us on the other side. Our persistent guides, shunting us through the maze of Acme Wonderland's many parking lots until we arrived at the entrance of Jubilee Town. Vale parked the truck. From here, we walked.

With no idea what to expect or how long we might be, we gathered guns and backpacks of food and water and ammunition. Vale yanked her overstuffed, bulky backpack on over her sleeveless back blouse, then swatted a mosquito away from the hem of her shorts. I wondered what she'd stuffed in there worth carting along. Birch tucked a notebook with a pen clipped to the cover into a pocket of his cargo pants, then smoothed the wrinkles of his Hawaiian shirt. I tugged off my sweat-stained T-shirt and replaced it with a clean, green concert shirt for a band I didn't know. I swept hair from my eyes, then wiped the sweat on my jeans and tucked my Beretta into the waistband at the small of my back. I grabbed my pack and slung it from my shoulders. The atmosphere of death thickened, imbued with cloying substance by the heavy humidity.

The turnstile awaited.

The dead lined the way.

When we entered Jubilee Town, they produced a horrible chorus of moans. An alarm? An announcement? Maybe a greeting? Whatever, it reached into my bones and filled me with cold dread. Icy perspiration crept across my back, the weight of my backpack plastering my shirt to my skin as it absorbed it.

Around us, shops and attractions offered delights and memories, all rotten and spoiled. Food overgrown with mold, overrun by insects. Toys and t-shirts caked with dust and mold. Photo rooms and novelty stores, abandoned. Places meant to inspire joy and imagination left to decay. No difference between this manufactured town and the many empty towns I'd passed through since escaping prison. Maybe the Red Man chose this place to send that message: no difference existed between the real and the imaginary. The real world held no more significance than a cartoon town deftly designed to move its visitors' money into the pockets of its creators. All societies, prison, the so-called real world, the microcosm of a theme park, even the apparent sanctuary of Miami, all of them charged a price, and all would one day die, cease to exist, rot, and decompose, and with time vanish from the earth, erased by history. Only death persisted. Only the dead knew permanence.

A headache exploded behind my eyes. I stumbled but kept on my feet.

"You okay?" Vale said.

"Yeah, fine," I said.

"You look pale."

"Pardon me for not sporting a hale and hearty complexion while we're walking through a theme park filled with walking corpses," I said. "I'll make sure I get my beauty sleep tonight."

"You don't have to be an asshole. I'm concerned, is all," she said.

"Thank you for that. Sorry. Sarcasm works wonders for my mood."

She smirked. "What, visiting the zippiest ol' town in the Storyverse doesn't brighten your day?"

"I was really hoping for cotton candy but looks like they're all out."

"That stuff will rot your teeth."

"Yep. Sweet, sweet poison."

I steadied myself, then resumed walking, passing Vale and Birch, who eyed me with a raised eyebrow and a face full of concern. I wished he'd share what was on his mind. Whatever the Red Man had done to him after Deadtown had changed him in a way I didn't understand. For the worse in many ways, yes, but it had also bred in him a steely resolve. Or indifference? Hard to tell. One way or another, Birch, as the saying goes, had no more fucks to give. Nothing made a man like him more dangerous to his enemies.

On the far side of Jubilee Town, the monorail station hummed with power.

The dead shepherded us there. When we hesitated to climb into the waiting car, they closed in, forcing us forward with their stench, their low groans, their nauseating presence. We boarded, took seats, and then the doors shut. A wormfeeder so rotted it resembled a dead tree stood at the front of the car in an Acme conductor's uniform, shirt unbuttoned. A cluster of eyes filled its chest, a line of them that ran up its throat to its face. Eyes stared from every bare scrap of flesh.

The monorail car jolted, then glided along the rail. I wondered where the power to run it came from. I wondered where it would take us. A goofy look came to Birch's face. He whistled the same song as me when we first went to meet the dead holy folks. *We're off to see the Wizard, the wonderful Wizard of Oz.*

"Wrong story, wrong universe," I said.

Birch didn't care. He kept whistling. Soon Vale and I joined in. Our conductor remained impassive.

Those eyes, though. The longer we whistled past their graveyard, the angrier they grew, and so we whistled louder, filling the car with that cheery melody as we rocketed over artificial towns and landscapes, observed by corpses, hurtling toward a cosmic darkness.

Ahead of us waited Storyverse Castle, glowing with an ugly red light.

The Red Man's light, the light of death.

We whistled louder still until the monorail stopped, and the doors slid open.

Crimson shadows enveloped us at the base of a wide flight of steps.

At the top, arched doors banged wide and stilted music poured out. A recording playing on damaged equipment, hissing, crackling, warped. The Storyverse theme song. Wormfeeders came from all sides and herded us toward the entrance. Vale shifted her bulky backpack, groaned under its weight, and started up the steps. Birch and I disembarked after her.

Connie Caribou greeted us at the peak. A decayed wormfeeder, dangling strips of flesh filled with wide eyes, she wore a filthy Connie Caribou costume head, outsized and askew on her scrawny neck and stick body, like a giant bobblehead, its fur-and-mesh eyes watching us from a cockeyed angle.

"Ugh, that's not right," Vale said.

"What?" I said. "Storyverse is for all good people who like good stories, ain't it? You saying the dead don't deserve stories?"

"Smartass," Vale said. "Connie Caribou was my favorite."

"Favorites die like everything else."

Vale glared at me. I felt bad mouthing off, but it eased my tension.

The castle doors led to the ride's boarding station. A giant crown car sat ready to take us for the tour of King Koala's Realm. Hidden within the walls, a generator growled, and motors hummed. A flashback to childhood nibbled at the edge of my thoughts. I ignored it. Childhood never looked like this.

Impatient, Birch pushed past me into the crown car and waved for us to get in with him.

We did, and I closed the door. The car bounced, spun twice, then glided into a dark tunnel filled with more warbling, distorted music. I knew the tune, the theme song from King Koala's Kindness Castle. Everyone knew that damn song. My brain filled the gaps, maddening enough, but when I saw Birch bopping his head to the beat like a happy Koala Kid, it left me dumbstruck. What the hell gears turned in that man's head? We all had our own agenda, our own story to follow, me, Birch, and Vale, three more loveable goofballs twirling through Storyverse's most memorable stories, from the first Connie Caribou cartoon to Polly Platypus's Puppet Parade that had ruled Saturday morning television for a decade, on to Captain Capybara's Conservation Comet educational films, and finally to the king himself. King Koala, who sat on the Throne of Tales with the Book of Good Stories by his side and ruled over all of Storyverse. I wondered if our names, our lives, appeared within its pages.

Only King Koala knew—except the Red Man had staged a coup.

Atop the Throne of Tales sat Darrell Philip Stradley.

In the Throne Room, our crown car stopped, then spun twice again before the whir of machines driving our ride died. The music played a few seconds longer, squelched by a final staticky crunch. All the Storyverse characters surrounded us, giant, mock heads mounted on hideous walking corpses, the worst, most decomposed I'd seen still mobile. On the throne sat the Red Man, bathed in light from the setting sun pouring through picture windows that overlooked all of Acme Wonderland. The Throne Room, meant as a showstopping moment on the ride, gave a vista of the entire fantastic realm. It hardly caught my eye compared to the Red Man ten feet above us on the throne pedestal.

He looked less dead than I remembered. His scars and wounds, so pronounced the first time I saw him, had faded. Not healed, so much as retreated from existence. His flesh looked supple, nearly alive. He wore the same tattered blue jeans and worn-out boots, now caked with dirt and dried gore. On his head sat an awkward crown, ripped from the head of the King Koala animatronic figure, which lay broken at the bottom of the pedestal.

For long, burdensome moments, no one spoke or moved. We stared at the Red Man; he stared at us, his crimson aura coruscating. A terrible stillness gripped us, gripped the world. The silence of death. Time seemed petrified, preserved, halted, the rippling red light emanating from Stradley the only thing in the world still animate and mobile. Then the Red Man cracked a wide smile, stood before his throne, stretched wide his arms, and cried out: "Welcome to my realm!"

He descended from the pedestal by stairs along the left side.

Vale tracked him with her rifle the whole way.

The Red Man walked right up and pushed the barrel of her gun aside.

"If bullets could hurt me, we wouldn't be here now, would we?" he said. "At one time, they did, but not anymore. Birch can tell you all about that. Right, Birch?"

Birch and I exchanged glances, both thinking the same damn question: When the dead rotted and the saintly dead held just this side of decay, how could the Red Man possibly look *more* alive than when we saw him in Deadtown?

He sat cross-legged against the edge of the pedestal.

"So glad you came. I knew you would. Sooner or later. By hook or crook." His voice grated with the tone of glass ground between slate. "Our unfinished business brought you here. My mark upon your brows made sure you survived the trip."

"I didn't know you liked cartoons so much," I said.

The Red Man's smile deepened. "Oh, I do, I truly do, because when I asked myself what better place existed from which to toss the final handful of dirt onto the coffin of the old, living world, no more fitting monument to the ephemera of life came to mind." He waved his arms, an expansive gesture to our surroundings. "All this means nothing, *never* meant anything. Yet the living flocked to it, worshipped it, wore its icons on their clothing and personal belongings, even their goddamn cars. They painted its gods on their children's faces. Dressed them in the robes and gowns of its high priests and priestesses. They mimicked its romance for their wedding rituals. It became a new faith. The religion of escapism, the dogma of the juvenile bolstered against ugly reality. Think about life's necessities: to eat, to sleep, to breed, the need for shelter and protection, the urge for connectedness, the drive to conquer our environment. A uniquely human experience, that last one, whether it meant curing cancer or shooting rockets to the moon. All that human energy, ingenuity, devotion, and joy, all that potential for grand accomplishment, diverted to things that never existed and never, ever will exist. Football games. Fashion shows. High-priced coffee. Social media. TV series and 24/7 opinion broadcasts. Life got so damn good people thought those things counted. They forgot where they lived. Forgot what it *meant* to live. They poured their obsessions into nonsense. Slaved for years to pay for two weeks in this illusory wonderland, a break from an already hallucinatory society where they lived day to day. How many places like this exist in the world? How many piped themselves into your eyes and ears day after day? How many false idols commanded the living's devotion? No small wonder when they died, their souls found the light that should've awaited them had given up and moved on. They killed their gods and heavens in exchange for false prophets and worldly paradises."

Vale raised her rifle, aimed it at the Red Man's face.

"You can shoot me, dear. I won't stop you. I won't enjoy it, and it'll mess me up a while, but I'll recover. I contain the power of a million dead souls. More flock to me each day. But, no, wait, on second thought, I'd hate to be shot by someone I've only just met." He extended a hand to Vale. "Darrell Philip Stradley, pleased to meet you."

Ignoring his hand, Vale pulled the trigger. Her shot passed to the side of the Red Man's head and bit a hole in the throne pedestal. Birch and I flinched from the report. The Red Man didn't even blink.

"My name's Vale." She lowered her rifle.

The Red Man withdrew his offered hand. "Truth be told, I already knew that. I know all about you. I've been piggybacking in your friends' heads." He stood and walked past our crown car to the royal banquet table by the windows. Six seats surrounded a table painted with a mural of Storyverse characters. The animatronic figures who'd once filled them lay cast aside on the floor. "Come, sit. We'll talk all about how you've come here to kill me and how you never had a chance at success."

Vale and I hesitated, but Birch exited the crown car, walked right over, and took a seat. It unnerved me how matter-of-fact he acted, but I also sensed method to his madness. We had little choice, anyway. Wormfeeders had gathered in the throne room and left us nowhere to go. Vale and I joined Birch and the Red Man at a table that looked like it belonged in a spoiled rich kid's bedroom.

"I like this place," the Red Man said. "You can see all the way to the entrance where you came in. See?"

The three of us absorbed the sight of Acme Wonderland beneath a pale sky so clear it looked painted. I squinted against a sudden blast of light as a fireball erupted with a cloud of smoke and flame. The picture windows rattled in their frames. The sound of the blast followed. When the thunder and rumble died, Vale walked to the window and stared at the burning patch on the edge of the park, the black plume rising to touch the sky—surging from the wreckage of Vale's truck.

"Shit," she whispered.

"You came here to kill me. Figured, hey, maybe if we blow him up, the fire and shock will use so much of his energy, his body will rot before it can repair itself. So, you filled a truck with explosives and hoped to get it near me. Of course, I had other plans. Not that it would've worked. I'm beyond even that now. The energy of each soul contained inside me sustains my existence. They come so fast, two arrive for each one I expend," the Red Man said. "You'd have to burn me for a year to destroy me that way."

"Vale, what the hell is he talking about?" I said. "Was that really your truck?"

She met my gaze for a moment then directed her eyes to the floor. "It was St. Bianco's idea. With the Red Man in your head, he figured we needed a plan you didn't know about."

"We drove all the way here in a fucking bomb?" I said.

"Yeah, sorry, I couldn't tell you," she said.

"Hey, hey, it's all right, Cornell. Women are entitled to their secrets. It's the mystery that makes them so intriguing," the Red

Man said. "That's what gets you hot for Vale, right? How much she reminds you of your lost love? You want to be with her, that's cool with me. I won't rat you out to that pretty little nurse you're making time with. My lips shall stay sealed. Hell, I bet Ms. Vale has plenty of secrets from her old life, things she's done to survive, things she'd be embarrassed for you to know about. She does adore you so, after all."

Vale swung her arm to slap the Red Man. He caught her wrist before she made contact.

"Care to share, darling?" he said. "No? Then sit the fuck down."

He shoved her toward a chair. Vale landed in it and hung her head low.

"You're all going to be part of my vision as I remake the earth. You, Cornell, shall be my right hand of justice. Your lady-friend shall be my left hand of wrath. Birch, my old pal, my dear murderer, my original assassin, my nemesis, in many ways, my creator, my father, my genesis, you shall be my pet."

"No." Vale slung the awkward backpack from her shoulders.

"You object, darling?" the Red Man said.

Fear spiked through me. Part of me, I think, had suspected St. Bianco's demand for me to go with Vale amounted to more than it seemed. Sparing a moment to consider it, even the secret truck bomb didn't completely shock me. When Vale peeled the backpack's top flap open, I felt more resignation than surprise. My anger flared, not for the betrayal but for the idea of never returning to Della and Christopher. Vale implored me for forgiveness, her eyes wide and gelid with tears.

"I'm sorry, so sorry," she said as she flipped the detonator switch on the bomb concealed within her backpack.

EIGHTEEN

My heart skipped several beats. My breath caught in my throat.

No explosion. No heat, no light, no concussion, no shrapnel to shred my body.

The switch clicked.

Vale flipped it again.

Click.

Nothing.

Click.

Nothing.

The Red Man laughed, and, fuck me, but it sounded exactly like the laugh of my old pal, my jackal, prowling forever in the back of my mind. My death in whatever form it may come for me one day. The only thing from which I'd ever run. The end of my world. It laughed at me. *He* laughed at me. Reminded me how I didn't matter, how little control I possessed over anything.

The Red Man seized the backpack from Vale. She offered no resistance.

Tears cascaded down her face.

"I know, I know," the Red Man said. "I cry too when my bombs don't explode."

He handed the pack to the dead. They passed it among themselves down the tunnel and out of our sight. I can't say I was sorry to see it go. Can't even say I was entirely sorry that it had failed because I was grateful to be alive. The Red Man daubed Vale's tears with a cloth napkin from the table.

"This power of mine lets me do all sorts of things, allows me to control the world around me," he said. "I give you credit for getting that package so close to me, but you had no chance of setting it off. Maybe if you hadn't shown it before you flipped the switch. Who knows?"

Groups of the dead approached.

"Enough talking for today," the Red Man said. "Go where the dead take you. We'll get together again, real soon, I promise."

"Fuck that," I said.

"Excuse me, Cornell, you say something?" the Red Man said.

"What are you going to do if we refuse? Kill us?"

Hate radiated off the Red Man. For me. For the living. For whatever corrupt and evil core thrived inside him and had led him to this point in his existence. That insight changed every-thing for me in the span of a single breath. The Red Man hated his dead self as much as he had hated his living self. Here stood a man who'd gotten what he truly desired and now de-spised what it made of him. Yet he couldn't turn his back on it, couldn't let go, couldn't walk away, and risk sinking back into a useless, pointless existence. Like all of us pushing onward through a dead world to survive, human maggots on a rotting corpse, he needed to keep moving toward a future, a new life, a new existence. He wanted to remake himself as one of the living and damn the world if he wasted it in the effort.

"Oh, I'll do much, much worse than kill you," he said. "Then I'll find that pretty nurse of yours and that dumb little orphan boy you took under your wing, and I'll do worse to them than I did to you."

I stood to go with the dead, not because of the Red Man's threats, but because now that I better understood his nature, I wanted time to make sense of it.

He nodded at me. "Good. Let's do this like we mean it. I used to guide the lost to higher levels of consciousness, to surpass their physical limitations. I'll do that for you. I can open the door to the universe's pure fuel and help you plug your soul right into it. When all our work here ends, and you ride high in the new world, you'll shower gratitude upon me."

He ascended his throne, pretending to ignore us as worm-feeders guided us to the outgoing tunnel. From outside the castle, another explosion came. Vale's backup bomb. He had let go, released control. Either it had moved out of range, or he could force his will upon it only for a short time, nothing permanent. Another hint. More evidence that the Red Man couldn't be all he seemed or wished to seem.

Ain't that always the way with the high and mighty, the ones who seek power, control, and authority, the ones telling everyone else how to live, how to think, how to view the world through the same compressed, myopic, and homogenous perspective. Bullies at heart, every last one of them, in search of socially acceptable ways to impose their will, to apply threat of force or social exile to alter our behavior. The Red Man simply killed the world to do it.

True leaders accept power rather than dedicate their lives to gaining it.

They manage it; they don't cling to it like mother's milk.

They don't see the world in the worst terms of *us* and *them*.

In that light, the Red Man seemed no different to me than an overzealous prison warden, or a ham-fisted sheriff, or a murderous saint, or any of the endless chain of people who'd tried to force me to live their way from childhood until the world ended.

Despite all his power and fearsomeness, he seemed small.

The dead brought us to underground cells for park visitors who broke the law at Acme Wonderland. Cushiest damn cell I ever occupied. Plush chairs. Cartoon murals painted on the walls. Even a bathroom stall with a door that closed. Probably intended to stave off lawsuits from anyone security held there until the police arrived.

The wormfeeders locked us in separate cells then left.

I couldn't see Birch or Vale, but I heard Vale crying. Birch started snoring, and I shook my head to think he could fall asleep under the circumstances. Of us all, though, he knew the Red Man, knew Darrell Philip Stradley, the best. Had known him in life and had spent those lost days of which I knew nothing with him after Deadtown. If our situation didn't frighten him, I took that as a sign hope still persisted.

"Cornell," Vale said.

"Yeah?"

"I'm sorry," she said. "Sorry I didn't tell you about the bombs. I would've blown us all to smithereens if the detonator worked."

"I understand," I said. "I hate it, and I'm pissed you lied, but I understand. St. Bianco wasn't wrong about keeping secrets from me and Birch to keep them from the Red Man."

"What he said about me and you, I'm sorry for that too," she said.

"What do you mean?"

A long pause preceded her answer. "I wish we'd met under different circumstances, in another world, maybe."

"In a different world, we'd be different people," I said.

No answer. Time passed. I lost track. The light never changed in our cells.

Fatigue overtook me, and I slept.

The dead did not bring us food or water. The Red Man did not visit, even in my dreams.

Right when I feared he'd decided to let us starve to death and fill our bodies with the souls of his followers, he appeared with an entourage of wormfeeders.

"Showtime," he said.

The cells opened. The dead guided us out, all three of us moving slow and unsteady from hunger and thirst. They took us outdoors to Royal Square in the shadow of King Koala's Castle, where a life-size cartoon horse figure sat, a prop for photographs. Despite their rotted-out limbs, their shriveled, caved-in faces, their bones poking through putrid flesh, their leathery muscles, tendons, and ligaments, the dead fulfilled the Red Man's orders like well-drilled soldiers. They held me and Vale on our knees. They stripped Birch to the waist then tied him across the back of the horse. The statue's oversized googly eyes glinted in the sunlight.

One of the dead handed a whip to the Red Man.

He lashed it across Birch's back.

As best he could without a tongue, Birch screamed.

"Death of the flesh to free the spirit, death of the spirit to free the flesh," the Red Man cried out. "Your preparation for my new world has begun."

NINETEEN

We spent days in agony.

Birch's torture kicked off a sequence of abuse and mortification at the Red Man's hands that would've brought a blush to the most jaded sadist. Each of us in turn, strapped to the cartoon horse, or tied down spread-eagled to a picnic table outside Foxy Pinewoods' Fish and Chips Hut, or chained to the back of a golf cart decorated like old Marvin Marmoset's jalopy pick up and run around the park till we fell and shredded our knees on the blacktop. At Andy Eagle's Aviary Adventure, he locked us in giant birdcages hung in the air from the steel and vinyl limbs of Elder the Oldest Oak and let us cook in the relentless sun, a feast for mosquitos thriving in the absence of the park's pest control management. Cut with blades, lashed by the whip, pricked with needles, dusted with salt that seared our wounds. We bled. Sometimes the dead lapped our spilled blood. Always each in our turn, and the Red Man made us watch each other suffer.

All day. In the heat and humidity. Our skin reddened and peeled. Our lips cracked from dryness. At night, the dead dragged us back to our cells.

Cartoon murals decorated our walls, like those in a pediatrician's office to make getting pricked for a vaccination or probed with a thermometer less horrifying to the five-year-old psyche. For us, it meant hours spent haunted by once-loveable characters transformed into harbingers of pain.

Always we found scraps of food and water waiting in our cells. No more than enough to sustain us until the next day. We only ate the prepackaged stuff, the bags of chips and sleeves of cookies, afraid of touching anything that might carry more than the taint of having spoiled.

On day four, I noticed the Red Man's daily decay.

Each morning, the wormfeeders brought us to him, almost as healthy as a live man, even a touch of red in his cheeks. Although his multitude of eyes betrayed him, he could've passed for a living man with bad skin when he closed them all. By the end of each day, purple and gray blotches appeared. His skin flaked and tore along its dry folds. His scalp thinned, stretched tight against his skull, paled, grew more skeletal.

Every day by sunset, he looked dead.

Next morning, alive.

"That bastard's restoring himself somehow," I said to Vale that night.

I lay on my cot, my body too riddled with pain for sleep. The rasp in Vale's voice told me she felt the same. Birch, on the other side of me, snored like an idling truck. I envied him that Zen center that allowed him to bear our tortures with so much equanimity. It simmered in the Red Man's eyes how deeply it burned his ass that Birch didn't beg for mercy and showed no fear after his first shocked scream on the back of the royal horse.

"What?" Vale said.

I explained what I'd observed; she'd noticed it too.

"I thought it was me, seeing things after all the shit he's put us through," she said.

"Nah, he's fixing himself using the souls he's gathered," I said.

"You know how that sounds, right?"

"No weirder than anything else I've said or heard these past months."

"You've got a point there." Rustling sounds came from Vale's cell as she shifted on her cot. Her voice trailed off, slurred, as she said, "How does that help us?" then fell asleep.

I didn't have an answer, but the question kept me awake a long time.

In the morning, when the wormfeeders fetched us for another torture-filled day at Acme Wonderland, I roused with the spark of a plan. I spent all day fanning its flames, ideas filling my head to blot out what the Red Man and his dead puppets did to Birch, to Vale, to me. When the day ended, I studied his face before our decomposing chaperones marched us back to our cells. The decay looked worse than at first glance. Cracks behind his ears. Lips sliding sideways. Eyebrows crumbling. Black spots on teeth that had gleamed white in the morning air. Across his chest, faint lines of old scars returning. The eyes that mottled his flesh drooped. It strained him to make himself look alive. Would the darkness make his restoration permanent when it arrived? Did he need the three of us to make that happen? No other reason to keep us around, wearing us down. I didn't plan to play along. If I couldn't figure out a way to destroy him, another option lingered in the back of my mind. He needed us alive.

That night, I jammed the lock of my cell.

I'd studied it every night, recalling all the locks I'd picked or broken in my old life, and rigged it so the door would close without latching. Not that the wormfeeders noticed. They had little awareness of their own. If the Red Man watched through their many eyes, fatigue made him careless.

I crashed on my cot. Ate the meager food left for me. Waited several hours.

No one came. No one checked my door.

Cut off from the outside, I had little measure of time. Trusting my internal clock, I stepped out of my cell at what I figured for the middle of the night. Birch lay sound asleep. Vale, too, tempting me to wake them up, but I had no way to get them out.

I backtracked our usual route to the Royal Square with the cartoon horse.

No wormfeeders in the underground security space, none in the plaza.

Weird. They didn't need to sleep. Night or day made no difference to them. Why not have them watch us 24/7?

In the western sprawl of the park, a red light glowed. I walked there, hidden in shadows. I knew my way around the park by heart, having run its full course so often while sucking exhaust fumes from Marvin Marmoset's jalopy.

I passed listless wormfeeders on my way to the brightness, which burned atop Polly Platypus's River Run. High up the ride, where the log flume shot out from a tight curve before plunging down a waterfall, a fire burned. No water ran along the artificial river. The chains and gears that pulled the flooms gleamed in the flickering illumination. Wormfeeders surrounded the base of the ride, hundreds thick, and so still I mistook them for part of the park until my eyes decoded their silhouettes. What I'd taken for fireflies were the flames reflected in their innumerable eyes, all open and staring at the top of the ride, beyond it at the sky, which possessed a darkness like spilled ink runneling among the stars. Some of the eyes watched the steel-and-resin hilltop. Others drank in that darkness.

The fire flared. Sparks and embers floated away into the night.

At the edge of the rail curve that arched into open air stood the Red Man.

Two wormfeeders brought him a body rotted beyond mobility. Its ragged flesh twitched. Its teeth and jawbone caught the light. From every part of it stared impossible eyes, each filled with dread and despair, apparent even across the distance between us.

The Red Man placed his hand upon the wormfeeder's dented forehead.

The act took a second, maybe two.

The ruined corpse sagged, lifeless, in the arms of the wormfeeders.

All the eyes upon it blinked shut.

A burst of red light flashed and winked out so fast I felt it at the back of my eyes more than saw it. New eyes appeared on the Red Man's body. His skin recovered a measure of its living luster; mottled patches of decay shrank.

As wormfeeders threw the wasted corpse over the side, another trio brought a fresh one. Something had sheared away half of this one's torso and most of its right leg.

The Red Man welcomed it, caressed its putrescent face. The transfer occurred again.

Crimson brightness strobed. New eyes opened on the Red Man.

Wormfeeders discarded the exhausted corpse over the side.

The darkness caught my eye.

Had it spread?

Had it reached down toward earth, attracted by the Red Man's acts?

Circles of blackness churned within it. Blind eyes whose gaze set my skin alive with a cold, electric discomfort. I felt seen and exposed.

I backed away from the River Run, retraced my steps, and returned to my cell.

Inside, unable to sleep, I wondered how to explain what I'd seen to Birch and Vale. When the wormfeeders came for another day of suffering, I still hadn't figured it out—but I'd decided before another night passed, I'd see either the Red Man or myself destroyed.

TWENTY

The Red Man always tortured us one at a time. In the moments he focused on Birch or Vale, I shared what I knew with the other and instructed each on how to rig their cell locks to stay open. When the wormfeeders left us that night, we licked our wounds, ate our meager rations, then waited a spell before leaving our cells. Despite her fatigue, Vale looked nervous.

"You have another hidden bomb we should know about?" I said.

"I wish," she said. "Just shaky from my daily beating."

"Might as well smile, then, because they'll continue until morale improves."

We all hung just this side of the living dead after the Red Man's torture. Indigo rings circled Vale's eyes. Birch's too. Pale and gaunt, they swayed on their feet. I knew I looked the same. We shared the weakness of suffering, part of the Red Man's strategy to grind away at us until we either begged him to stop and agreed to anything he wanted, or lost ourselves so deeply we came to believe in him, brainwashed. We would last another day, maybe two or three at most, before we died from deprivation and the slow blood loss that came each day. I'd never break. I stared death in the face now and found it familiar and inevitable, my personal jackal waiting to laugh me along the path to oblivion. I hoped Birch and Vale would hold out to the end if it came to that, but you never knew how one might crack when their life lay on the line. As if to answer my unspoken question, Birch offered me a folded piece of notebook paper from his pocket.

I took it from his trembling hand, unfolded it, and read the words written there in wavery but legible penmanship.

Scenario 17

Death of the flesh to free the spirit = Releasing souls, life force, spiritual consciousness? Energy cannot be created or destroyed. The anima of life enters a void of their making, a pool of genesis energy, a vitality battery, a limbo-container that shields it from... what, from its return to the cosmic biofilm of matter and energy, its dispersion to stardust?

Death of the spirit to free the flesh = An exchange, a price, a sacrifice, the anima of the captured souls expended to "free the flesh." From what can flesh be freed? Aging. Mortality. Decay. The spirits given over to it make the flesh eternal, incorruptible. Who/what accepts the payment and grants the boon? *The Darkness.*

I lifted my gaze from the paper. Birch regarded me with such hope and yearning for me to understand what he'd spent hours pondering and working through in his notebooks. As if the theft of his voice had been a blessing that allowed him to focus his brain entirely on decoding whatever Darrell Philip Stradley hoped to achieve. Vale read over my shoulder.

"What's that? What's this mean?" she said.

Birch gripped my arm, squeezed, implored me to comprehend.

"I think," I said, "that the Red Man is trying to become fully alive again, that he needs to be alive for the darkness to make him... immortal?"

Birch nodded as he wept. Tears streaked his cheeks.

Yes, yes, yes.

"What happens if he does that?" Vale said.

Birch gestured, miming an eruption, things sweeping away, the end of everything.

"Nice pep talk, buttercup," I said.

Birch cracked half a smile through his tears.

"Scenario 17," Vale said. "What are the others?"

Birch shook his head, shrugged them off, tapped the paper in Vale's hand.

This is the one.

Vale returned the page to Birch, who refolded it into his pocket.

"Makes as much sense as anything," I said. "Doesn't help much with killing Stradley."

Be patient, Birch conveyed with his hands and expression.

The park's underground corridors ran in all directions like ant tunnels. Last night I'd spied an access door near Polly Platypus's River Run that let us avoid the wormfeeders on the surface. Stairs led to the door, emerging into an alley alongside the River Run gift shop. The smell of decay blasted us. We crept to the alley's end and spied the gathered dead. High up the River Run, the Red Man stood on his perch. The expanse of night sky writhed with darkness. Low and close now. Like storm clouds creeping in fast from the horizon, erasing blue skies and sunshine, stars and moonlight. The darkness felt low enough to touch, as if it would soon reach the ground and envelope the earth, maybe tonight, maybe a couple of nights from now, but soon.

Vale grasped my shoulder.

"Promise me," she said, "if you see a chance to kill the Red Man, you'll take it."

"That's the whole damn point," I said. "What's gotten into you?"

"Nothing," she said. "Just, if I can give you that window, you'll take it, right?"

"Dive through it headfirst. Likewise?"

"Yeah. Good." Vale clasped her hands to my face, drew me into an unexpected kiss. Her cracked, dry lips rasped over mine. Her breath tasted sour, but the contact, the surge of living warmth, the intimacy, the affection brought a moment's pure bliss before Vale broke it off. "For luck." She pushed past me out of the alley.

Birch flashed me a stupid grin like some goofy high school freshmen

I blushed. "You want a kiss for luck, don't look at me."

The three of us skirted the edge of the wormfeeders to a path that dead-ended against the edge of the River Run. We hopped a fence and landed in thick hedges, where we dropped to our bellies and crawled. We'd agreed to climb up inside the River Run in hopes of taking the Red Man by surprise. Our way through the faux mountain proved harder than expected, climbing narrow ladders and catwalks and stretches where we walked the ride's exposed rails, feet sliding, hands grasping at whatever hold presented itself. We met no wormfeeders. All of them, except for the handful serving the Red Man, stood below. The Red Man's ego made him cocky. He needed those bodies, those millions of unnatural eyes cast up at him, at the darkness speeding across the cosmos to touch him. Their worship made him the holy man, the leader he believed himself to be. The righteous savior of the dead. Herald of a greater, universal truth than anyone had ever revealed to the masses. Their devotion measured his power. Sent a message to the darkness and all the lost souls contained in rotting flesh that he could take them anytime he wanted, that they served him, not the other way around. He wanted them to know it, needed them to believe it.

Needed them to believe it.

Needed...

The power of narcissism.

It amazed me how much of Stradley's living psyche remained intact after dying.

What did that say about all the dead holy folk sitting on their hotel-lobby thrones back in Miami, all the supposed "good guys" in this battle between light and dark, all the similar groups of dead and living, who—if St. Bianco spoke true—played out final acts like us? People who demand you live according to *their* needs, who needed you to pretend *their* fiction equaled reality, for *their* benefit. And so very many people eager to comply.

I saw little difference between the dead who filled Acme Wonderland now and the living who'd filled it in the past. So easy back then for anyone to buy a life, a reality, a philosophy, a prefab set of values and opinions. Subscribe here. Join a tribe. Pick your favorite media flavor with a side of politics, religion, outrage, and bonus professional sports team and film franchise. Receive their daily newsletter beamed direct into your head. Enjoy ready-made thoughts to live by. Waste no effort generating your own. Take no time away from living your best life to think.

You get convenience; they get control.

St. Bianco exploited human vulnerability no less than the Red Man.

Saints. Sinners. Two sides of a coin of entitlement and aggrandizement.

The only escape: reject it all, carve your own path.

Ignore the sales pitch. Deny the programming.

Rob a fucking bank and stick your finger in society's eye.

Push past fear and comfort until you broke through to the other side: freedom.

Trust that knee-jerk reaction against the authority of the appointed, the cruel corrections of the mob. As much as people hated and feared me in my bank-robbing days, admiration and envy complicated their emotions. They wanted me caught and stopped for breaking the law and bucking the established order—but really, for showing them what living life on your own terms looked like and shoving their complacency in their faces.

For the first time in days, the laughter of my old friend, the jackal, lapsed mute.

Maybe he didn't like my line of thinking. Maybe he figured I no longer needed him to goad me to self-destruction. Maybe he shut up because I grasped the world in a way I hadn't ever before and that we—that *I*—might really be part of a cosmic design that transcended us all but never forgot us. Then and there, I sensed it in my skin that we *could* resist the darkness—and the *Darkness*. We mattered. Each one of us. Every individual. Our decisions and actions mattered. All the choices I'd made that led me here had been right, no matter how heartbreaking.

Yet, despite my newfound awareness, I still saw no way to destroy the Red Man.

We reached the last ladder, ascended, and came within sight of him.

A dozen wormfeeders surrounded their leader. Three tossed a corpse drained of its lifeforce off the side of the resin-and-steel mountain. Three more brought another broken shell, a man in the tatters of an American flag t-shirt. Fear burned in its dozens of wide-open eyes.

Truth revealed.

The genuine end of a mercilessly prolonged existence.

No heaven or hell awaited. No oblivion.

Only the anger, obsession, and desire of the one who guided them back and warehoused them in rotting flesh. From the ground, a million or more eyes stared, unperceiving.

Rot tainted the Red Man's not-yet-fully-restored face.

"I was wondering if you might join me," he said. "I've enjoyed our dance, but if you listen real hard you can hear the music winding down now. The party's almost over."

Behind and above him, Darkness ruled the sky.

Red light flashed. All the flag man's eyes turned glassy and shriveled as the life behind them entered Darrell Philip Stradley. The darkness thickened. A whip of utter black unwound toward the Red Man then snapped back to the sky.

"More," the Red Man said. "Bring me more."

From the base of Polly Platypus's River Run, the masses of the dead moaned.

"Death of the flesh to free the spirit, death of the spirit to free the flesh," he said.

The Red Man ingested more souls from another fractured corpse. Its putrescent flesh vanished over the side, landing on a growing pile. He smiled as the flush of life returned faintly to his skin then raised his arms to the black sky and made a sound I can't rightly describe. A scream, a roar, a cannon shot blasting from his throat, a deep reverberating bellow that erased all other sound. It filled our ears, rattled our bones. The world rippled in its sound waves. Now the Darkness sent three coiled whips of its void skin to caress the Red Man's face then withdrew them. Stradley dropped to his knees and cried out, a human sound this time, of anger, defeat, fatigue, and frustration. A crack in the façade of his power.

So close, yet fallen short, he struggled too.

"Another!" he shouted.

Wormfeeders brought him the legless body of an obese woman, terrified eyes staring out from every fold of its decayed skin. I couldn't see this last night, this fear in the eyes of the dead, the reality of Stradley's transactions with his reanimated followers. His desperation. Their final understanding of how he'd manipulated and used them.

Birch shoved a crumpled paper in my hand: **Scenario 17.**

A flash of red. Another spent corpse dropped to the bottom of the River Run.

The Red Man repeated his inhuman cry, channeling some resonance from the foundation of reality, then he reached for the sky, for the Darkness, which reached back, and brushed his fingertips before it vanished.

Birch took more pages from his pockets.

Unfolded them.

Showed us each one briefly before casting it over the side of the synthetic mountain.

Scenario 2. Scenario 23. Scenario 7. Scenario 4. Scenario 13. Scenario 18. Scenario 32.

All filled with his quavered script. Cast to the gentle wind. Snowing down on the dead. Fluttering across their eyes.

He poked the paper in my hand.

This is the one.

Stradley's followers in life had bought his bullshit about freeing themselves and his followers from whatever hell-afterlife he'd created to hold them, bought it about coming back to life. He had conned them all. They believed him because they had no other choice. Too late for questions now. Trapped. They signed on for the world he promised them, one that wouldn't—*couldn't*—ever exist. A world of ghosts and hollow promises.

"He's using the dead to power himself by taking their souls," I said. "They make him almost alive again, but he can't hold enough to bring himself all the way back. The Darkness needs the living."

A rotted arm flew at us, landed by our feet. We all flinched.

"Are you watching?" the Red Man said. "Tonight I become the world. This is your last chance to join me in the new reality. One way or another, I'll make sure you take it."

A flash of red, another corpse spent, and the Darkness reached lower, lingered longer brushing across Stradley's livid flesh.

Vale stepped forward. "Why us? Of all people, why us?"

The answer came as Stradley groaned at the loss of contact with the Darkness.

Freedom.

The dead have no choices.

Trapped in his promises.

Only the living retain free will.

"He needs us to choose," I said. "To push himself over the threshold, he needs the anima of people who join him of their own choosing. He's let us live because he sees that possibility in us. He's threatened us, bullied us, tried to bribe us to buy into his horseshit. We give him energy from living flesh, the Darkness can enter him, and then he becomes immortal. We become like he is. Dead, incorruptible, but tethered to him forever, always at his mercy. Another fucking prison. Ain't that right, Stradley?"

Birch raised his hand, three fingers held up.

He nodded his head, then lowered one finger.

Two fingers. He shook his head, then lowered another finger.

One finger and another head shake.

Reading Birch's meaning, I said, "He only needs one of us to succeed?"

Birch nodded. Message delivered, he shut his eyes. The exhaustion and trauma he'd hidden since Deadtown showed all at once. He looked one step this side of dead; he looked un-burdened. Vale, on the other hand, looked reenergized. And me, dancing around the obvious, I still saw no way to use what we knew to destroy the Red Man. Like the old saying goes, I was so close, if it was a snake, it would've bit me—and that's exactly how it felt when Vale spoke what my mind refused to see. A bite. Venom pumped into my blood. Death at my vision's edge. Even then, my thoughts only circled the truth.

"I'll join you," Vale said. "I want to live forever in the new world."

TWENTY-ONE

Vale's words sank in while Stradley flashed red, absorbed another batch of souls, and flirted with the Darkness.

"You understand now," he said after the Darkness withdrew. "Death of the flesh to free the spirit, death of the spirit to free the flesh. Whoever among you makes the sacrifice shall stand with me forever in my favor. I welcome you, Vale. I welcome all who come to me of their own free will."

I studied the other's faces, rage at Vale flaring inside me. Vale, an outsider, always alone, who I barely knew, but reminded me so much of my first true love. Vale, who'd tried to blow us to smithereens. I opened my mouth to speak, to say... what? I don't know, because before a word crossed my lips, Vale punched me square in the face, hard enough to rattle my brain and send clouds of stars and darkness across my eyes. I staggered into Birch, who caught me as best he could, crumpling to his knees, both of us winding up on the deck.

Vale stepped up to the Red Man.

"The men aren't worthy," she said. "They want the world back the way it was. They don't deserve the gift you're offering. They don't deserve to serve you."

Stradley's face lit with the smug self-satisfaction of being proven right. In his mind, it had only been a matter of time. Vale's words cut me, though. Deep. To my soul. Her voice brimmed with conviction and certitude. No trace of doubt. She chose the new dead world that had peeled back the curtain on her own self and set free the person hidden inside her for so long, one of the old-style living dead, with prefab lives and minds. She turned her back on that world, that existence, and I can't say I blamed her, but I couldn't forgive her for trading it in for the version Stradley offered.

My head spun as I struggled to my knees.

I stumbled and dropped to the ground again.

Birch tried to help me, my dead weight too much for him.

Stop Vale.

Get back on my feet. Steady my head.

Grab Vale. Kill her before she reaches the Red Man.

I couldn't pull myself together.

Blood ran from my nose, filling my mouth with metallic saltiness.

Birch and I braced against one another, clambered upright together.

The stars in my eyes faded to after images.

My head settled.

Pain cleared my thoughts.

"Vale, no!" I shouted.

I took three steps, only to stop when everything resumed spinning.

How hard had she hit me? Not that it took much after days of torture wearing me down.

I rubbed my head and shouted again. I'm not sure the words made any sense.

Vale paused, glanced back at me.

"Let me open the window," she said.

She knelt at the feet of the Red Man. He placed his hands on the sides of her head. Red light flared, brighter, burning with the intensity of pure life—first life—putting to shame the energy trapped in dead flesh. The flash seemed to go on forever, filling my eyes, blinding me—and then it intensified. I looked away, to the sky, where the red light penetrated the Darkness. I saw inside it. How can I explain what it contained? The Darkness wasn't monolithic, nor a single entity, nor a cosmic toxic cloud, nor an absence. It held multitudes of faces within faces within faces. Eyes within eyes within eyes. Infinity rolling out in fractal waves of shades of black and deeper black and the black of nonexistence. It churned with violence, hate, and chaos. Jets and sparks of black energy flared within it, visible only as black lightning currents. It made no sense how I could see any shapes, any features in that festering hegemony of darkness. They imprinted on my perceptions over the blank canvas of the Darkness, my brain rationalizing madness into a form it could comprehend—and it *hurt*. My brain swelled against my skull. My head throbbed with an ache like a thousand migraines.

Beside me, Birch dropped to his knees, stared at the sky, let it flow through him as he accepted the experience.

Vale screamed.

The Red Man roared.

No longer deep down in the back of my mind but right there at the surface, my jackal laughed—and I knew he saw something I hadn't yet perceived.

The red light faded. Ropy darkness twisted toward the Red Man.

He looked alive, hale, hearty, and full of life.

Full of life.

Life.

All life dies.

The impulse exploded inside me, so urgent and overwhelming, my body responded before I knew I was in motion. I rushed Stradley. I passed Vale's prone figure, passed the slow-moving wormfeeders, and hit the Red Man with my full weight, slammed him against the faux rocks and scrub brush alongside the tracks, steamrolled him out of reach of the Darkness, which lashed at the empty air where he'd been standing. Thrusting my legs, jumping, pushing, I carried us both over the side and into empty air.

If I can give you that window, you'll take it, right?

Dive through it headfirst.

Vale hadn't turned her back on us at all.

Stradley screamed, the first time ever I heard fear in his voice.

Instinctually, I thrust my hands out, seeking hold, finding the rough edges of sculptured vinyl, fingertips scrabbling to change my momentum. I swung hard against Polly Platypus's mountain. The wind rushed out of me, but I jammed myself into a crevice that stopped my plummet.

The Red Man found no such luck.

His body hit the ground, the thud and snap of it music to my ears.

For long seconds, the dead stared at him.

He sputtered blood from his lips, tried to rise.

Tried to stay alive.

Alive among the living dead.

It dawned on the wormfeeders slowly, but they figured it out soon enough.

Another living piece of meat to satiate their appetites.

They descended, ants to a dropped ice cream cone.

One more scream.

The Red Man's light failed.

Stradley vanished under corrupt flesh.

He *died.*

Birch helped me back to the ride's high outcrop.

The wormfeeder servants ignored us and descended, hoping for their share of the flesh of the man who'd lied to them.

We could do nothing for Vale, who'd sacrificed her life to empower Stradley and allowed the Darkness to make him mortal for the crucial seconds we needed to kill him before he attained immortality. The Darkness boiled in the sky. Cheated, it frothed and raged. Black whips snapped from it and lashed overhead, unable to touch us. A door Stradley had opened had slammed shut with his death. For a time, Birch and I sat, Vale's head cradled on my lap, while the Darkness stormed, and the wormfeeders sang their awful song of death and need to a deaf universe. Vale did not reanimate. Whether from St. Bianco's blessing or because killing Stradley had changed the equation in our little part of the world, I didn't know. I felt no less gratitude or grief for it, though. When the Darkness finally spent itself and fled the sky, a shaft of morning sun broke through the clouds and painted Vale's face so pallid and empty, a part of my heart broke for her. I slung her body across my shoulders in a fireman's carry. With Birch's help, I navigated the long descent through the mechanical innards of Polly Platypus's River Run. We emerged into sunlight and an electric tension I'd only ever felt before in the moments after a hurricane passed, revealing the full measure of its devastation.

Not only had the wormfeeders turned on the Red Man, they'd turned on each other.

Hundreds of them lay in broken shambles everywhere. Squirming limbs ripped from torsos. Broken bodies writhing on the earth. Viscera puddles sending ripples of steam into the humid morning air. Heads lolling as mindless jaws snapped and ground. Hands, even individual fingers, worming across the hot pavement. The dead had torn themselves to pieces, echoing the tumult and fury of the Darkness. Or in a conscious act of self-destruction to free themselves from the trap into which Stradley had tricked them. Or for some other reason I'd never know, could never understand. One thing about that charnel debris, though, struck me with amazement and the first real spark of hope I'd experienced in longer than I could remember.

From not one body, limb, spilled organ, or scrap of flesh did an eye look upon us.

The souls trapped in the dead were gone.

Only flesh remained.

Death of the flesh to free the spirit.

With the truth of how Stradley had used them revealed, the dead, when given a choice, threw a honking, big middle finger at the Red Man and whatever Darkness he courted and put themselves back to rest on their own terms.

"Hey, you hear that?" I said.

Birch eyed me, confused, and shook his head.

"That damn jackal isn't laughing anymore."

Confusion wrinkled Birch's expression, but I gave no further explanation. Any words I might've spoken would've been cut short anyway by the eruption of a white light from the perch atop the River Run. My chest clenched tight, fearing The Red Man had somehow returned, and I know Birch's did too. We heeled about, shaded our eyes, and peered into the brilliance. Instead of the Red Man, though, another figure stood there, light flowing out of him: St. Bianco. He looked down upon us, raised his hands in a gesture of... affirmation, blessing, congratulations? Who knows what goes through the mind of a saint? He vanished a moment later, but the light remained. It settled over us like a mist dropping from the sky. As far as we could see in every direction, the dead ceased moving. That light finished the job they'd begun. An unexpected sense of relief filled me. My mind still doubted, but my instincts knew some great part of the conflict between the living and the dead, the light and the Darkness, concluded in that moment—and in favor of the living.

I shifted Vale's weight on my shoulders. "Going to be a long road back to Miami."

Birch nodded, then together, we took the first step.

LOHATCHIE CODA

One morning, a pillar of black smoke stabbed the clear, blue sky.

I sipped coffee on the front porch and watched it billow, unfurl, and expand into a brown haze staining the sky over the town to the east, figuring its source for the intersection of Lohatchie's Main Street and Banyan Road. That raised my hackles, though I couldn't say why exactly. Nor could I guess the cause of the smoke. No one lived in Lohatchie anymore. Far as I knew, only me, Birch, Christopher, and Della lived within a fifty-mile radius of town, and the reanimated dead don't set fires.

The front door creaked open then clicked shut behind me as I eyed the smoke. Della slid an arm around my waist, leaned into me as she sipped her coffee. "Spontaneous combustion?"

"Fires like that don't set themselves," I said.

"Wormfeeder cookout?"

"Only if the wormfeeders are the ones getting cooked. The dead may be dumb, but they know not to play with fire."

I laced my arm around Della's shoulders and kissed her on top of her head, inhaling the scent of sleep still lingering on her hair. Her body warmed me in the morning air.

"Well, if it's not the dead and fires don't start themselves," she said, pausing to sigh, "we got company in town."

"There goes the neighborhood," I said.

Green and brown surrounded us. Sawgrass filled the spaces between cypress, mangrove, and mahogany trees, broken by colorful splashes of wildflowers, even a few orchids south of the house. The green buzzed and chirped, abundant with wildlife. The sawgrass swayed where unseen critters traveled. Less than a mile west of our place ran a river that flowed out to the coastal marsh, and the most motion around us came when the wind rustled the trees. A Toyota SUV in desperate need of a wash sat in front of the house, windshield still peppered with dead bugs from our last scavenging run into Lohatchie.

More and more time passed between each trip now. The town had little left to offer, and Birch's garden out back brimmed with vegetables year round thanks to his clever planning. Christopher and I brought in plenty of fish and game, and in time, the apple, lemon, and orange trees we'd planted would add to the bounty. It amazed me how well we could live off the land in the absence of competition and civilization. Paradise. A pocket of vibrant life on a dead earth. My Lohatchie hideaway delivered all the things I'd hoped for when I first set my sights on her in the early days of the dead plague. The road here took its toll, sure enough, but this scrap of a home carved from the green wild worked a kind of healing magic on us all. After every terror and torture we'd survived, we needed it. Hell, we deserved it.

So that column of smoke dispersing itself toward the heavens?

That tightened my chest and put tension in my brow.

The sight of it gripped my heart in a stony fist.

It reminded me of another darkness, one spreading itself across the cosmos—one I hoped never to see or contact again. And until now, I believed in that possibility. But such is this world that no matter where you go, no matter how you live, the darkness always finds a way to catch up with you.

"I'll wake Christopher," Della said.

"Let him sleep a little longer. He's a growing boy," I said. "Nothing to gain by rushing. Enjoy the morning. No telling how things will look this time tomorrow."

Della's arm tightened around me. With Miami a year-and-a-half in our rear views and the Red Man destroyed, the dead he'd rallied to torment us lost their way. They still roamed the world, but with less aggression and no purpose. The souls inside them that looked out through the eyes that pocked their corpses seemed to be winding down and losing coherence. We'd almost come to take for granted the predictability and routine of life on the edge of the Everglades. I knew better, but it still stung for that pillar of smoke to shatter the illusion.

I finished off my coffee, hugged Della, then walked inside.

Birch slept on the sofa, his body so long, his feet hung over one arm. He laid so still with his arms folded over his chest it creeped me out. He looked dead. Worse, when I kicked the sofa leg and barked out his name, he didn't move a muscle, only opened his eyes, rising from slumber instantly. He levered his legs around and sat up. Ran a hand across the gray stubble on his scalp, the dry skin of his palm scraping, then shot me a questioning look.

"There's smoke in town. Where there's smoke, there's fire. Where there's fire, there's..." I said. "Well, me and Della think we got company. Better we scope it out before they find us here, so we keep this place our little secret."

He nodded then stood and flashed me an open hand. *Give me five to get ready.*

Once we found time to heal, I'd hoped he'd find a way to regain his voice, lost when the Red Man ripped out his tongue, but he remained as silent as ever. I left him pulling on his boots.

My place outside Lohatchie, passed down from my great-grandfather, consisted of a living room, kitchen, two bedrooms, one bathroom, and a dirt-floor cellar, where we kept our guns, ammunition, and other weapons scavenged along our journeys. Funny how so much of it accumulated after we destroyed the Red Man and stopped getting into constant scraps with the dead. Without his influence, the wormfeeders lost their will and dispersed. St. Bianco, who possessed the power to still the living dead, did so for all those in the Red Man's inner circle of ghouls at Acme Wonderland, but, I guess, he couldn't swing it for all of South Florida. They still troubled us, but at least they no longer swarmed or forced us to fight for every inch of road. We ran circles around them now. If we avoided them, they ignored us. Whatever bond once drove them to hunt us no longer existed.

We hardly ever fired a gun or bloodied a blade these days except when hunting. Other dangers existed out there, though, as they always had. I preferred to face them well-armed. I gathered handguns, rifles, and shotguns, a crossbow, knives, hatchets, a slingshot, with which Christopher could take a crow out of the sky, and lugged it all upstairs to load in the SUV.

Birch, returning from taking a leak on the edge of the wild, helped me load them.

I slammed the hatch shut.

Birch nodded to me. *Good to go.*

Christopher emerged from the house, dressed and ready to roll, except for his hair mussed in six different directions of bedhead mayhem. Della followed. They hesitated a moment to study the distant smoke. Christopher yawned, but then his eyes narrowed with irritation at the intrusion into our solitude. None of us relished routine more than him. That's what the young need, if only for something to test and rebel against—and I'd noticed the signs of rebellion growing in him as he hit the age when boys commence figuring out how to become men. Good for him. We all took that path sooner or later, if we lived long enough.

We climbed into the SUV in silence.

I cranked the engine, circled us around, and rolled up the trail toward town.

The closer to Main Street we drove, the more wormfeeders we saw.

Only in ones and twos, though. They no longer traveled in mobs, flowing like rising whitewater.

They barely noted our passing. The numberless, unnatural eyes that pocked their bodies showed fewer signs of life with every passing day, as if the souls behind them clung to existence in a process of slow decay, their vitality fading, the hungry gleam they once turned on us dimming under a milky haze. They didn't care anymore about what had once burned so fervently in them that it enabled them to persist after death, return to the world in borrowed flesh, and prey on the living. How that worked or what they hoped to gain, I still didn't fully understand, but I gladly accepted their weakening.

I guided the Toyota along a side street lined with empty houses and parked half a block from the main road. We slipped out of the car, armed ourselves from the trunk, and then broke into two teams.

Birch and I strolled toward Main Street. Christopher and Della headed to the other end of the block to move in along Biscayne Road, parallel to Main Street, backing us up while keeping out of sight. The rank odor of burning rubber tainted the air, emanating from the heavy, greasy smoke forming a shroud over the town. At the corner, I crouched and peered around the side of a long-abandoned hardware store, most of its useful goods now stored at my place. Fire raged at the far end of Main Street. A car burned. In its open trunk a pile of tires seethed with heat and smoke. Maybe a quarter mile away, yet the heat tickled my cheeks. I withdrew, let Birch take a look.

"I didn't see anyone," I said when he pulled back and straightened.

He shook his head. *Me neither.*

"So why burn tires and a car in the middle of the road? No point other than to catch someone's attention, I'd say, because it makes one hell of a mess. Impossible to ignore." I scanned Birch's impassive eyes, saw no objection. "Which means they're assuming someone is here to see it. Or, worse, they *know* someone's here to see it."

Birch nodded.

I reached into my pocket and plucked out the handset from a pair of walkie-talkies Christopher had collected from the hardware store. I'd laughed at the time, but they'd come in handy hunting and even around the house. Smart kid, that one.

I kept my voice low as I held the transmit button and spoke into it: "Someone definitely set the fire on purpose. We can't see anyone, though. You in position? Over."

Seconds passed before Della came back. "We're on the west corner of Banyan and Biscayne, a block down from Main. We don't see anyone. No one living, at least, but we got a couple wormfeeders taking root in someone's front yard across the street. Over."

Taking root. What the wormfeeders did when they ran out of steam. Found a place out of the way then stood there and rotted to dust. It took a long time. I knew of "wormfeeder graveyards," where they clustered like living grave markers waiting to disintegrate. It paid to stay alert around them, though, because sometimes they sprang back into action in a resurgent burst of hunger.

"Watch 'em close. Don't turn your backs on 'em," I said. "Birch and I are taking a walk. Squawk if you see anyone living. Over and out."

In silent agreement, Birch and I stepped around the corner, moved into the road, and walked right up the middle of Main Street at a Sunday-stroll pace. Birch carried a .45 in his right hand, low at his side, a .30 caliber rifle slung across his back. I cradled a 12-gauge shotgun in my arms, my 9mm holstered at my waist. We each wore a knife and a hatchet tucked into our belts. Walking up Main Street in plain sight might seem foolish, but time and again I'd found the direct approach worked best when confronting strangers. Anyone who knew enough about us to want us dead would've known where to find us. We had no living enemies, none we knew of at least, and it paid to make a show of ownership, striding through town like we alone belonged here, no one else.

The closer we moved to the fire, the worse the smoke and stink grew, until my eyes itched and watered. We halted about a hundred yards from the torched car, glanced around, saw no one. The car sat right in front of Mona and Joan's, a diner and ice cream shop back in the day.

A voice I'd forgotten whispered in my memory.

French fries and strawberry shakes.

"Shit," I said. "It can't be. No fucking way it can be."

Birch raised an eyebrow. I ignored him.

"All right, we saw your smoke signal. We came. We're here," I shouted over the crackling flame. "You going to make us wait all day?"

My gaze darted from one doorway to the next, one rooftop to another, from shadow to shadow, seeking a man I'd never expected to see again, near seven feet of muscle and meanness I'd watched die. Or at least thought I had. I held my breath, waiting for him to step out of a patch of gloom into the sun and firelight. Instead, a smaller, far-more surprising figure appeared.

A girl, maybe twelve, thin, gangly, wearing ill-fitting clothes, dirty brown hair tied back in a ponytail, ash smudged on her face, emerged from Mona and Joan's. She eyed me and Birch with fear. The two of us stared back at her for long seconds as we processed the sight of her.

Finally, I said, "Hey, there. We won't hurt you. Do you need some help?"

She nodded then vanished into Mona and Joan's.

Birch raised his left hand, palm up, snapped the first two fingers of his right hand against it, then closed a fist around them.

A trap.

"Sure feels like it," I said. "At the same time, it doesn't."

Birch raised both eyebrows at me for that.

I shrugged. "Feels like something else, that's all."

I reported to Della over the walkie then, with Birch's silent resignation, approached the door to Mona and Joan's. The fire warmed the back of my neck. Its smoke spilled around me. I covered my nose and mouth with my hand. Birch coughed then did the same. We waited a few moments for our eyes to adjust to the shade inside the diner then pushed the door open and entered, carrying our guns, ready.

"Hey, there, Lohatchie boy. Long time, no see," a man said from the back of the diner.

That whispering voice given full volume.

Seated on one of the counter stools, he shifted his mass, putting his face into the light. I blinked several times, making sure I saw who I thought I saw. He looked scarred and thinner, no less powerful or muscular than I remembered, and at the same time, faded and withdrawn, his deep brown skin tinged gray as if he'd sunken deep inside himself, taking refuge in the shelter of physical prowess—but that had changed even more than I realized at first. I understood fully what my eyes told me when he stood. He had lost his left arm, from the shoulder, and a scarred, ragged stump protruded from his sleeveless, muscle shirt.

"Fuck," I said. "Last I saw you, it looked like the wormfeeders had torn open half your chest."

"Damn near did. Wound up smeared in so much dead gunk the others gave me up for lost and left me alone long enough to squirrel out of there. Hid out until the hornet's nest shitshow we started ran its course. You're one mean son of a bitch, Cornell. Anyone ever tell you that?"

"Who keeps track?"

Birch tapped my shoulder, glanced from me to the man and back again.

"Birch, meet Klug, aka the King Snake. Klug, meet Birch."

Klug spun on his stool, showing off his cobra tattoo. It covered the back of his bald skull and ran down his neck, along his spine, and under his shirt. "Hey," he said as he rounded to face us again. Birch said nothing. "Quiet type, huh?"

"Can't speak. Someone took his tongue," I said.

"Ouch, my sympathies, brother," said Klug.

"Yeah, I'm sure he appreciates that. You two can be the charter members of the Lohatchie Lost Appendages club." My shock surrendered to tension. I changed the pitch of the shotgun in my arms. Klug didn't overlook it. "I suppose you set that fire for a reason."

"Sure did, and you ain't gonna need that scattergun," he said.

"I have vivid memories of pinning you to a wall with a truck, then the two of us trying to get each other killed by wormfeeders while I stole the getaway keys from your pocket."

"I remember that too. Wild times, man, wild times. The things we do to survive. Who can blame us?"

"You saying all is forgiven?"

"That's exactly what I'm saying. Not only that, but you were right."

"I was?"

"Yes, sir. We should've stuck to the plan and broken out of that prison. You got no concept of the hell that place became after you ditched it with Della and Mason. One of those 'life-altering' experiences people used to jaw about back when there were still enough people to listen. As Warden Lane Grove might've said, 'The scales fell from my eyes.' That and months and months of surviving second to second without a left arm changed my outlook."

"How so?"

Klug gestured to the girl. "You already met Chloe."

"Hi," she said, her voice shy, hesitant.

Two other children crept out from behind the counter. A black boy half Chloe's age, clinging to a superhero plushie at odds with the defiant look on his face, and a black girl, almost a teen, wearing a belt of knives, her hair cropped close to her scalp. The two bore a family resemblance.

"Meet Merit and his sister, Tayna," Klug said.

I nodded to each one and spoke their names. "I'm Cornell. This is Birch."

"Hi," they said.

"All of you now, come on," Klug said.

"It's like a damned clown car. How many you got hiding back there?" I said.

"Only them and Nina. Let's go, girl. No one here's going to bite you," Klug said.

A girl of fifteen or sixteen and several months pregnant revealed herself, rising behind the counter as if she expected to need to take cover again at a moment's notice. She wore a dirty, blue sundress and stared daggers at me with her brown eyes.

"I ain't the father," Klug said. "That was Rennie. Lost him about a month back."

"What the hell is this, Klug? You running a mobile daycare?"

Klug chuckled. "Like a halfway house on wheels. Della still with you? If she is, they all could use a look over from a good nurse. Nina's gonna need all the help she can get in a few months. It's why I came here. That and my yearning for one last strawberry-and-banana milkshake. Not going to get that, though, am I?"

"I am at a loss," I said.

"I was too for a long time," Klug said. "Things changed the first time I found myself around kids who needed protecting." A frown soured his haunted face. "None of those first ones are here. I did what I could. We can only do so much in this fucked-up world. We all got our limitations. We all come to the end of our road one day. I'm getting to mine. I thought, well, where in this whole, wide, savage world could I leave these four that they might have a chance without me? I figured if you were smart and tough enough to outdo me back in prison, you might have made it all the way to Lohatchie. I liked the idea of coming home too. Don't have time to wander the neighborhood knocking on doors, so I figured I'd send up the signal. You'd have to come if you saw it because we can't afford mysteries in our own backyard these days, right? I underestimated you once, not again."

I found no words to respond. The children watched me with intense, curious stares. Klug had guided them to a turning point, but they didn't know which direction their lives would take from here. Klug stared at me with different questions. The kind I thought could never even occur to a man like him, who'd lived his whole life by force, intimidation, and treachery before the dead plague, a man who did everything he could to deserve the name King Snake. Merit stepped to Klug's side, reached up, and took Klug's hand. Klug's massive, knobby fingers wrapped around the boy's with a gentle touch I'd have considered beyond his capacity. Like me, Della, Christopher, and Birch, though, Klug had defied the odds on more levels than one.

I raised the walkie to my mouth. "Della, meet us at Mona and Joan's. We're inside. We've got some kids who need a little nursing. Over."

A crackle of static, then Della came back, "On our way. Over and out."

"Got something to show you," Klug said.

He gestured for us to go out the back door to the small parking lot behind the diner. The sickness inside him revealed itself when he rose from his stool. He hunched over, his right hand clutched against his belly, and winced at the pain from whatever ate away at him. He took a second to catch his breath then shuffled along to the door. Despite his frailness, my gaze roved over him, seeking weapons. I saw none, but old habits die hard, and trust doesn't wink into existence because someone surrounds himself with children.

I traded glances with Della, who paused examining Nina long enough to notice how bad Klug looked. She'd already checked the other kids and given them clean bills of health, except for their hygiene, which we could remedy easily enough, but Nina filled her with concern, and that worried me. She nodded the okay for me to go, though, so I did. Birch came along behind me as I caught up to Klug. Christopher started to follow too, rising from where he sat playing cards with Merit, Tayna, and Chloe. I waved him off. I wanted him backing up Della, wanted to spare him whatever Klug had in mind, because I couldn't imagine anything pleasant waiting for us.

Klug opened the back door. We stepped into the sunlight of a day on track for high heat and humidity, the kind of day when we got up early to finish all our chores so we could spend most of it in the shade of our porch. Across the parking lot stretched a garden of the rooted dead, casting shadows in unison like giant-sized sundials. I hadn't been this way on our last few runs into town and had no idea so many had planted themselves here. They took no notice of us as far as I could tell. The breeze twitched their ragged clothing and disintegrating hair. Some of them swayed a little as it blew.

On the sidewalk that ran along the asphalt square sat a red cooler stained with dirt.

"Check this out," Klug said.

He toed the edge of the cooler lid then flipped it open with a kick. I don't know what I or Birch expected to see in there, but neither of us could've guessed the reality: a dead arm squirming on the cooler bottom, a dozen eyes blinking from its rotting flesh. The eyes squinted at the sunlight suddenly permitted into their nest. The cooler barely contained the big limb. It wriggled like a lizard dying staked to the ground by its tail, until the proverbial light bulb switched on in my head, and I directed my gaze at Klug's stump.

"Fucking wild, right?" He laughed, but it turned into a horrible, hacking cough. It took him almost a minute of wheezing to get his breath back. "I keep it as a reminder of how easy it is to lose things we take for granted in this world. Get me? I have this connection to it, to the dead through it, like a window into what they know, what they want. Let me tell you, that shit has kept me up many a night. It don't make a lick of sense, but it's helped me stay a step ahead of them when it mattered. Like an early-warning system. Now, though... now, they don't hardly seem to care much about anything. Like they're winding down. You notice that?"

I gestured to the still figures that filled the parking lot. "I see it all the time."

Klug looked over his shoulder. "Yeah, true. Maybe that's what's killing me. Whatever's passing out of them is passing out of my arm and draining the life out of me too. Or maybe it's just cancer eating my insides. Who knows? Don't make it hurt any less or change the result. I got only so much strength inside me, and when it's all eaten up, I'm gonna be right there with them."

Klug flipped the cooler lid closed. It snapped back open, making all three of us jump.

"Oh, shit," Klug said.

Pain burdened his voice. Like a knife thrust into him forced the words from his mouth.

The dead fingers of his severed arm curled over the lip of the cooler. The hand flexed, dragging itself up. It spread its fingers, opening its palm, full of winking eyes, and shook so forcefully the cooler rattled on the ground. Those eyes hadn't paled at all, preserved and sustained, perhaps, by their link to Klug's living energy.

In the parking lot, the wormfeeders roused. Despite their aimlessness and decay, the dead sometimes still traveled fast. In the blink of an eye, they turned to face us, then took rough, shambling steps in our direction. A few toppled over, their bodies incapable of motion on bones too brittle to support them and muscles, ligaments, and tendons long-since shriveled and snapped. One, whose feet seemed glued to the asphalt by putrescence, dropped as its ankles cracked. It tried to crawl, but then its wrists cracked too, leaving it stranded to wriggle its stumps on hot blacktop. The mob of them emitted a discordant, collective groan, as if anguished over their return to motion.

"The fuck is this?" I said.

Birch tugged on my shoulder, drawing me toward the door.

I resisted, fascinated by the dead uprooting themselves, wanting to understand what had sparked them back to motion. Birch pointed at Klug and yanked on me again.

Klug blinked his eyes several times and swayed on his feet. His jaw rose up and down, and his lips quivered. They looked like smears of ash. He couldn't catch or hold a breath. For a moment, his hand clung to the side of his gut, where his pain seemed to originate, then it slid away and hung limp at his side. I still didn't get what Birch had already sussed out.

"Birch's right. Let's get back in inside, Klug," I said. Klug didn't reply, didn't move. I dropped my hand on his shoulder. "Let's go, man. Come on!"

The King Snake heeled around to regard me with empty, glazed eyes. A gurgling moan escaped from his throat. A death rattle. He lunged his right hand at me, trying to grab my face. I fell back against Birch, ducking Klug's reach. Birch and I bolted to the door, no need to drag me along now, the two of us bumping together as we rushed inside, and locked it shut behind us. Dead flesh pounded against the wood, but it held.

"Fuck me, did he just die on his feet while we were talking?"

Panting, his eyes wide, Birch nodded. *Yeah, looks like it.*

"Ain't that a stitch?"

We hurried into the diner.

"Time for a hasty departure," I said. "Gather everyone up. We're going for the SUV."

"Where's Klug?" Tayna said. Her hands rested on the hilts of the knives strapped to her belt.

"Klug's out back in the parking lot. He was a lot sicker than you knew. A man that strong can hide a sickness for a long time. Keep himself going like he's better off than he really is. Then it catches up with him all at once. That's what he did to get you all here, keep you safe. But he's not sick anymore. Do you understand what I'm saying?"

"Liar! I don't believe you! You did something to him. He said you wouldn't be happy to see him. You hurt him! What did you do?"

Tayna's expression turned feral. She moved in a blur, unsheathing one of the knives at her waist and throwing it, missing my face by inches so the blade sunk itself into the wall behind me. She grabbed Merit's hand and pulled him along as she dashed out the front door.

"Come back," I called out.

Della and Christopher jumped up to run after them. I stopped them with news of the dead in the parking lot. "There could be others out there rousing for a last gasp. Seems like Klug's death set them off, like whatever life went out of him restarted their engines. We need to be careful."

"So what's the plan?" Christopher said.

"Della, Birch, you take Chloe and Nina to the SUV, lock them inside, and protect it. Christopher and I will find Merit and Tayna and meet you there," I said. "Then we get the hell out of town."

Christopher cracked the door and poked his head outside. "All clear."

We exited Mona and Joan's, the thud of dead fists against the back door fading behind us.

The heat and smoke from the fire turned the street to hell. That car would burn a long time.

Della and Birch led Chloe and Nina away toward the SUV, moving fast but with caution, keeping the two girls between them. I gestured to Christopher, and we walked the other way, rounding the fire as close as we dared as we crossed the street. I looked for signs of which way Merit and Tayna had run but saw no hint. They might as well have vanished like ghosts.

"Merit said they stashed their car nearby," Christopher said.

"Did he say where?"

"No, only said his sister did the driving because Klug couldn't anymore. Klug told them where to park because he grew up here."

Weekends, holidays, Main Street in Lohatchie filled up with people running errands or enjoying the town, parents taking kids for ice cream, teenagers cruising, people on their weekly gossip-and-shop route. The parking lot out back of Mona and Joan's and every other under-sized lot filled up fast on those days, which meant street parking for latecomers. Smart locals often went for that first anyway because two nearby streets offered easy parking in the shade while the sun cooked the public lots, and it gave them an edge on the traffic when it came time to leave. Klug had grown up here. He had to know about that.

"I got an idea where to look," I said. "Follow me."

Christopher walked beside me to the end of Main Street. The road continued, but shops gave way to houses. A mile farther down, if we were to walk that far, it gave way to nothing but sawgrass and trees, but no one ever parked down there. We passed the first residential side street, Finlay Road. No cars, only a handful of the dead rooted and rotted in front yards. On the second road, Chestnut Street, my guess paid off.

A Cadillac Town Car sat halfway down the block, neatly parked in the luxurious shade of an old red maple tree. The dead surrounded it, pressed against it, pawing at the windows, groaning, struggling to find a way inside, where Merit and Tayna clung to each other in the front seat. Why hadn't they started the car and driven off, I wondered. Echoes of the past provided the answer. They didn't have the keys; Klug did. Probably in his front shirt pocket like he'd had the truck keys so long ago back in the prison of Warden Lane Grove when I'd stolen them from him and escaped.

The yards along Chestnut Street had comprised a few wormfeeder graveyards. Many of them had uprooted themselves to pursue the kids. The others remained planted in place, their eyes noting us, watching, but indifferent. Their deteriorated bodies swayed, from the breeze, or maybe excited by the action at the car. I figured a good number of the dead had wandered over from Finlay Street too. Dormant for so long, until Klug rang their alarm clock.

"There's too many to dodge or kill," Christopher said. "What do we do?"

Merit and Tayna spotted us. They slapped their palms against the windshield and screamed for us to *help us, save us, get us out of here.* Just kids, dumb enough to throw a knife at me in one moment then beg me for help in another.

The smart play would've been to walk away, rendezvous with the others, and head home. Leave behind what amounted to two more mouths to feed, that's all. No one had asked Klug to bring a bunch of kids here, to trust me to take them in. But he had. Down to his last breath, my enemy came to me for help. Once, we'd tried our best to kill each other. You couldn't say either of us had defeated the other, but we'd persevered. Beyond that, though, the look on Christopher's face made the smart thing to do an impossibility. His expression removed "walking away" from my lexicon of moves. He intended to solve this problem. He needed to save those kids as he'd once been saved. I refused to let him down.

"We shoot them, we'll be ringing the supper bell for the others out behind Mona and Joan's, over on the next street, hell, anywhere around here. That only gets us cut off from the SUV." I pointed to an Acura with four flat tires in a nearby driveway. "Hide yourself behind that car. I'll draw them off the Caddy. They'll scatter a bit when they come after me. I'll lead them the other way. Once it's clear, get the kids out and head back the way we came for the SUV."

"No way, you can't dodge that many," Christopher said.

"Don't worry about me. They're slow, old, and unmotivated. I won't have to dodge them all, just a few of the overachievers, I said. "Besides, I got a plan."

Christopher met my gaze. I didn't turn away. I needed to sell the lie, couldn't let him see it in my eyes that I had no plan except to play rodeo clown for the wormfeeders long enough for him to retrieve Merit and Tayna. That's what parents do: They make sacrifices for their children. Put themselves at risk for their survival. Give of themselves. I wasn't Christopher's father and never really would be, but there was a time when I would've been a father. A time before prison, death, the dead plague, and mad saints ruled a world sinking into decomposition. A time when long-dead Evelyn, who blessedly passed before all this insanity, would've made parents of us both—and I let her and our baby die, taking all the hope I'd ever had of living a normal kind of life with them.

This time, I promised myself, it would go differently.

Once Christopher hunkered down behind the Acura, I rampaged at the Caddy.

I skidded to a stop and poked one of the wormfeeders with the tip of my shotgun barrel. Then another one. I prodded a third, a fourth, then onward, one after another until half of them noticed me and scraped their attention away from the kids. I howled and whooped and jumped around, mocking them, keeping myself out of arm's reach and glancing over my shoulder to check the ones still rooted in the yards. Most of the wormfeeders, about a dozen, left the Caddy and trailed me as I led them like the Pied Piper leading rats. I guided them beyond the Caddy, toward the far end of the block. When they slowed, I darted in and poled the frontrunners. A few lingered at the car, dead faces pressed to the windows. I grabbed a rock from the ground and threw it at them. Another. One more. I hit them in their faces, aimed for their multitude of eyes, made them see me. The curb tripped me, and I almost fell, but the tactic paid off. The last three joined the free-lunch crowd hoping to eat me.

"Go, Christopher, go, now!" I shouted.

On the other side of the Caddy, Christopher appeared, running so hard he stopped himself by slamming into the driver's side door. He slapped at the glass, urged Merit and Tayna to unlock the door, get out, run with him. After several horrifying seconds of fumbling, they did. They scrambled free of the Caddy, too frightened to argue now, and bolted with Christopher. I watched them turn the corner and dash back along Main Street, out of my sight.

Left alone with fifteen wormfeeders, I evaded their clumsy assaults.

When I reached the next corner, I stepped from the proverbial frying pan into the fire.

A mob of new admirers more than twice the size of the Caddy crew approached from the direction of town, likely formed by uprooted wormfeeders from Mona and Joan's parking lot. They had missed out on their prey at the diner, but they'd caught the signal.

Come down to Chestnut Street. We got fresh meat.

It's a block party for the dead.

Chowtime, soup's on, get it while it's hot.

Or at least warm-blooded.

The two groups melded together, a handful of wormfeeders falling as they tripped over each other. None rose again. The others simply stamped them to a gory mush on the street. I backpedaled, stringing them along toward the road out of town. They came faster than I expected, but not fast enough to catch me. With Della and the kids on their way to safety, I hoped and prayed, I raised my shotgun and let loose into them. If the report drew more of them my way, so much the better. Each blast did much more damage than I'd expected. The rooted ones weren't sturdy. They were the difference between uprooting a healthy tree and a dead one. The former makes you work for it; the latter rips right out of the soil. Several wormfeeders collapsed in the road, bodies so disrupted by shot, they no longer functioned. Enough kept coming to worry me. I crept backward, firing a shell every couple of seconds. More dropped and lay in the street like earthworms dying in the sun after a rainstorm. The stragglers slowed. An end to my pursuit appeared. I reloaded the shotgun, fired four rounds in rapid succession, knocking down a seven-ten split of wormfeeders. The last two didn't worry me. Their knee bones showed through their broken dead flesh, clicking, sliding like gears out of sync, on the verge of failing.

"Enjoy the rest of your walk, folks," I said.

I heeled around and ran, intending to rush up the next side road back to Main Street and hook up with the others. Instead, I bolted into a solid mass of dead flesh and muscle, hard enough to stagger me back two steps.

Klug.

He stared me down with a hundred eyes, but his own milky set sent the worst chill through me.

His right hand swung, almost slow-motion, and easy enough for me to dodge, but I felt the wind from it and knew it would punish me if it landed. He stumbled closer, took another swing. I ducked, lost my balance, fell to the ground, and rolled with the motion, coming up on my ass at the curb. The two wormfeeder stragglers hooked up with Klug. The trio moved on me, the way Klug had so often moved on his enemies in the prison yard, with backup, a gang, the implication of overwhelming numbers, a show of force to remind you of your weakness. Except Klug's intimidation, dead or alive, no longer sent a chill through me. Back when I met him, I'd wanted to stay clear of the web that people like him use to draw you in and manipulate you, but I'd learned how impossible this world made that. No one stayed clean, no one walked away free—not unless you fought for it.

"Shit, Klug, look how far you came, saving kids, and making peace with me, and now, you're right back where you started, you fucking evil, deadhead bully," I said.

I didn't try to rise to my feet. I braced the shotgun to my shoulder and fired.

The recoil slammed me flat on my back.

Scrambling onto the sidewalk, I watched Klug's decapitated body wobble. The blast had vaporized his head, neck, all of what remained of his left shoulder, and most of his right. His one arm bobbed from a thread of tendon and ligament.

The stragglers moved past him. I stood, steadied myself, and blew their faces away too.

"Son of a bitch, Lohatchie just ain't what it used to be," I said.

Groans and the rasp of air whispering through dead flesh caught my attention. More of the dead came shuffle-stepping in my direction. Another sound reached me too. A car engine.

The SUV came bouncing and jolting across a nearby front yard as it swerved out of a side street, rounded a cluster of worm-feeders, and skidded to a hard stop. The passenger door swung open. Tayna leaned out from the passenger seat. A chorus of voices yelled at me to get in. Jumping into the SUV, I shoved Tayna onto the console between me and Della, behind the wheel. I yanked the door shut behind me then pulled Tayna onto my lap.

Della floored the gas. I counted heads in the back seat. Everyone there.

Christopher crouched in the trunk, covering our six out the back window. Merit and Chloe sat on Birch's and Nina's laps. I never saw so welcome a sight. Our little group, or unit, or family, or whatever the hell you called it, had just doubled in size, and something about that fact that I couldn't put into words made all the chaos and death around us fall away like scenery.

"Took you all long enough, kid," I said.

"You shut up before I throw another knife at you," Tayna said. "We saved you didn't we?"

"That you did. You saved Klug, too. No matter how he died, you did that for him in life. I hope you know that." I let out a long breath. "And I hope you like gardening."

Tayna flashed a questioning eye at me. I didn't bother to explain. Plenty of time for her to learn, for all of us to learn.

THE DEAD WON'T DIE

As of the publication of *The Eyes of the Dead*, I've lived in the Corpse Fauna world for twenty-five years. If you define the modern zombie as walking dead ghouls who feast on the flesh of the living versus traditional voodoo zombies and place their birth in 1968 with the release of *The Night of the Living Dead*, that's just short of half the lifespan of this most popular of 20th-century monsters. Back in 1997, when I conceived the first story in what grew into the Corpse Fauna cycle, a dedicated fan could have, with a little effort, seen all the modern zombie movies—certainly all the ones worth seeing—and read all the modern zombie books and comics. There were *no* TV shows. That last fact is hard to fathom today when there are, as of this writing, three series about a world plagued by modern zombies currently on the air, more announced to come soon, and several more available through streaming services. More remarkable is the unfettered torrent of zombie movies that shamble forth on a regular basis from all over the world.

With all this attention from creators and audiences, though, does the modern zombie still matter?

The godfather of the living dead, George Romero, imbued his tales of flesh-eating ghouls with social commentary, using reanimated corpses to weave satire and pointed observations into his movies. Many people once considered that element an essential ingredient of the modern zombie mythos, yet, that aspect has faded with time. Just as Bram Stoker's commentary on Victorian sexual mores in *Dracula* has faded from vampire stories. Even as Mary Shelley's themes of humanity's relationship with its creations and discoveries have faded from adaptations and retellings of *Frankenstein*. In many ways, the modern zombie now stands with werewolves, mummies, and slashers as merely one more menacing figure in the pantheon of horror tropes and cliches.

With all due respect to the many excellent stories of modern zombies told since 2005, it's tempting to declare the modern zombie complete and fully formed as of the release of *Land of the Dead*, George Romero's fourth and final film in the original Dead series. He followed it with two more movies, *Diary of the Dead* (2007) and *Survival of the Dead* (2009), and even continued to build on his ideas in various comic book series, such as *Toe Tags* and *Empire of the Dead*; an anthology, with Jonathan Maberry, *Nights of the Living Dead*; and a novel, with Daniel Kraus, *The Living Dead*. All of those explored ideas and possibilities in the world of the living dead, but few of them added substantially to the idea of the modern zombie or to its full realization as a true classic monster. That George accomplished in *Land of the Dead*.

The classic monsters, as defined in film and fiction, include ghosts, Frankenstein's monster, mummies, werewolves, vampires, and even the Creature from the Black Lagoon. What they have in common and what makes them classic is how they not only represent universal fears but that they exist as fully rounded characters, monstrous and frightening, true, but also sympathetic and imbued with humanity. We regard them with more than fear, with perhaps even sympathy and compassion. Consider the romance of Dracula; or the tragedy of Frankenstein's monster, shunned by his maker; or the vibrant, charming Lawrence Talbot afflicted by a beast within him beyond his control; or the Creature, a lonely prehistoric throwback upon whose tranquil home eager scientists intrude. We find something in these monsters to love or, at least, with which to empathize, an aspect, characteristic, or circumstance that makes them as interesting to audiences and readers as the human characters who confront them. In some of those classic stories, the most monstrous character isn't the creature but the humans around it.

Most of the classic monsters possessed those elements from their introduction. They sprang to dark life fully formed in their debut novels or films. For modern zombies, though, it took four movies made over a span of more than twenty-five years to get there. In *Night of the Living Dead*, the "ghouls" acted as little more than assassins. Random. Inexplicable. Single-minded. Blind appetites driven by mindless hunger. A mob overwhelming resistance from the living through thoughtless persistence and sheer numbers. With *Dawn of the Dead* (1978), they evolved into mute stand-ins for the worst traits in modern humanity. Consumerism. Materialism. Mindless adherence to convention. Then in *Day of the Dead* (1985), they exhibited the first signs of consciousness surviving death—or perhaps new consciousness emerging after death. As though resurrection of the body cat-alyzed a rebirth into which a new consciousness entered. All fascinating stuff in a sense of monster and world-building, shedding pure monstrosity for something more meaningful—but not yet on a par with the classic monsters that came before.

Another twenty years passed before Romero took us there in *Land of the Dead*, which fulfilled the vision the filmmaker had expressed decades before as the ultimate goal of his *Dead* movies. In *Land*, the dead show all the signs of having become a rival branch of humanity, a mutant species, fighting for their survival, even for the dignity of their new mode of existence. They become sympathetic like the classic monsters. Humanity must still fear them and cannot coexist with them because, no matter if we might understand their will to live and recognize their undeniable—though inhuman—consciousness, they still want to eat the living and make more of the dead. In *Land*, the mod-ern zombie becomes the underdog triumphant. Audiences could finally root for these monsters and sympathize with their urge to live their undead existence to its fullest. Thus the modern zombie took its place among the pantheon of the truly classic monsters. As in all of the Dead films, there are far more monstrous humans in the story.

Romero took a long and roundabout path to that point with his creation—but the silver lining came in the form of four incredible horror films made at distinctly different points in history, allowing each to resonate in a different way and reach new audiences. Yet the question remains: Does the modern zombie still matter?

Are all stories of modern zombies since 2005 really about post-modern zombies? The challenge of working in a post-modern mode is to find new perspectives and themes in a thing considered complete and fully rounded. To breathe new life into creations so familiar they no longer evoke much of a reaction in their well-known form. To reinvent them.

What of Corpse Fauna, a series of novellas and stories that spans the modern/post-modern eras?

That has been one of the greatest challenges in writing these stories, publishing and republishing them, spending intense periods of time with these characters, then taking long vacations from them, then back again like a family reunion with your grimmest group of old friends. A strange experience. Some of the initial inspirations for Corpse Fauna seem less compelling to me today than they did when I began this story cycle. Some seem more important than ever. The theme of social authority and control versus individual freedom, identity, and will, which runs through all the stories, resonates even more for me today. So does the notion of an ambiguous power fueled by thousands or millions of trapped souls that watches and strives to control one's every move, every choice, every thought. And the challenge of simply being left alone to live one's life in a world where the masses feel entitled—even compelled—to interfere with the lives of people to whom they have no real connection. I leave it to my readers to ascertain what these ideas relate to in the real world.

In this sense, I consider the Corpse Fauna stories modern zombie stories, not post-modern, positioned squarely in the sweet spot Romero left open to those of us who cared to enter it in the zombie drought years between 1985 and 2005. Back when modern zombie stories were expected to be about more than mere survival, and the zombies needed to function as more than a generic threat in stories and movies that fit better into the sub-genre of survival horror than zombie fiction.

Still, does any of this answer the question? Does the modern zombie still matter?

It matters to me. I suspect it matters to my readers. For all the love of movie magic, special effects, and unforgettable characters that have made post-modern zombie stories, movies, and television shows so entertaining, the living dead seem a bit hollow without those essential elements that made them great in the first place. As long as writers seek those greater possibilities in what makes the modern zombie such a fascinating classic monster—and as long as readers and audiences continue supporting it—the modern zombie will continue to matter. And matter more than the post-modern zombie.

Coming to the end of the Corpse Fauna cycle with *The Eyes of the Dead*, I realize I've inadvertently followed even more closely in Romero's footsteps than I'd ever intended. It's taken a quarter-century to bring all these stories to publication and complete what I envisioned many years ago. There have been a number of false starts and setbacks not unlike those Romero experienced seeking funding for his Dead films. Yet here I am, having reached the end of the story (or the end for now...) because the Dead truly *won't* die—unless we let them.

I owe a tremendous amount of gratitude to all those readers who have followed Corpse Fauna's winding and circuitous path and its many resurrections. Your interest and support made these books possible. Thanks as well to the wonderfully supportive and professional folks at NeoParadoxa and eSpec Books, who not only provided the opportunity to fully realize what I'd imagined for Corpse Fauna but have gone above and beyond to make it the best it can be. A very special thanks to two artists who have been part of this journey with me: Glen Ostrander and Jason Whitley. I'm finicky about how artists visualize my characters and concepts, but Glen and Jason, apparently, can read my mind. Their interpretations and representations of Corpse Fauna have been pitch-perfect every time, and their enthusiasm has helped keep me going on the long trek from "Prison of the Blind Dead" (read my afterword in *The Dead Bear Witness* if you don't know what that is) to *The Eyes of the Dead*.

Thank you for reading.

—James Chambers
April 2022

ABOUT THE AUTHOR

James Chambers is an award-winning author of horror, crime, fantasy, science fiction, and other genres. He wrote the Bram Stoker Award®-winning graphic novel, *Kolchak the Night Stalker: The Forgotten Lore of Edgar Allan Poe* and was nominated for a Bram Stoker Award for his story, "A Song Left Behind in the Aztakea Hills." *Booklist* described his collection *On the Night Border* as "...a haunting exploration of the space where the real world and nightmares collide," and, in a starred review, said of his collection *On the Hierophant Road*: "For fans of the new breed of dark-speculative-fiction writers who actively play with genre confines to create reads that are inventive, thought-provoking, and creepily fun." *Publisher's Weekly* gave his collection of four Lovecraftian-inspired novellas, *The Engines of Sacrifice*, a starred review and described it as "...chillingly evocative..."

He is also the author of the short story collection *Resurrection House*, the Corpse Fauna novellas, including *The Dead Bear Witness, Tears of Blood,* and *The Dead in Their Masses,* as well as the dark urban fantasy, *Three Chords of Chaos,* and *Kolchak and the Night Stalkers: The Faceless God.* His short stories have been published in numerous anthologies, including *After Punk: Steampowered Tales of the Afterlife, The Best of Bad-Ass Faeries, The Best of Defending the Future, Chiral Mad 2, Chiral Mad 4, Gaslight and Grimm, The Green Hornet Chronicles, Kolchak the Night*

Stalker: Passages of the Macabre, Qualia Nous, Shadows Over Main Street (1 and 2), *The Spider: Extreme Prejudice, Truth or Dare, TV Gods, Walrus Tales, Weird Trails,* and the magazines *Bare Bone, Cthulhu Sex,* and *Allen K's Inhuman.*

He edited the Bram Stoker Award-nominated anthology *Under Twin Suns: Alternate Histories of the Yellow Sign* and co-edited *A New York State of Fright: Horror Stories from the Empire State,* also a Bram Stoker Award finalist.

He has also written and edited numerous comic books including *Leonard Nimoy's Primortals,* the critically acclaimed "The Revenant" in *Shadow House,* and *The Midnight Hour* with Jason Whitley.

He lives in New York.

Visit his website: www.jameschambersonline.com.

ABOUT THE ARTISTS

Glen Ostrander (cover) is a Freelance Artist and Illustrator who has created artwork in the fantasy/horror genre for a wide variety of commercial clients. He is known for his evocative work and continues to bring his creations to life by finding daily inspiration near his home, in the wild mountains of New Hampshire, where he lives with his wonderful wife Anna, his devilish dog Jojo, and his fiendish feline Floyd.

Jason Whitley (interior) is the illustrator and co-creator of *The Midnight Hour*. Jason's work as a newspaper illustrator has appeared across the country and won many awards. His portrait of civil rights leader Charlotte Hawkins Brown is in the Charlotte Hawkins Brown Museum.

With writer Scott Eckelaert, he co-created and illustrated the classic comic-strip, *Sea Urchins*. Sea Urchins has been collected into four volumes. The fourth volume, *So Long, Frozen Ocean* will be released in 2020. Jason leads a Hermes and Telly Award-winning multimedia team of five in North Carolina. He's working on a crime-noir graphic novel with no set release date and looking forward to the complete *The Midnight Hour* collection from eSpec Books in 2023.

OUR LEGION
OF THE UNDEAD

ABD
Agnomaly
Amy Grech
Angela Yuriko Smith
Anna Taborska
Annelise Pichardo
Anonymous Reader
April Grey
Arthur Kinsman
Aven Lumi
Avis Crane
Becky Wood
Bill Ginger
Brian W. Matthews
Carl W Bishop
Carlos Valcarcel
Carol Mammano
Chandler Klang Smith
Charles E. Wood
Cheri Kannarr
Chris Ryan
Christopher J. Burke
Cori Paige
Craig Hackl

Curtis Steinhour
Dale A. Russell
Damon Griffin
Dan Dalal
Danielle Ackley-McPhail
David Swisher
Diane Raimonde
Drew Biehl
Drew Cucuzza
Dusk Zer0
Ef Deal
Fiona A. Elder
Frieda Schultz
Gail Trotter
Gary Phillips
Giusy Rippa
Hank Blumenthal
Howard Blakeslee
Isaac 'Will It Work' Dansicker
J.R. Murdock
Janet Lees
Janito V. F. Filho
Jeff LaSorsa
Jenn Whitworth

Jennifer L. Pierce
Jessica Sarchet
John L. French
Jonathan Lees
Jp
Karen M
Karl Markovich
Kierin Fox
Kirk Larson
KJSP
L. E. Daniels
L.E. Custodio
Lakota Lara
Lara Frater
Lark Cunningham
Laurel Anne Hill
Laurie Jones
Lisa Kruse
Lisa Morton
Liz
Lorraine J. Anderson
Lou Rera
Lynne Hansen
Mallory N Pate
Mandi
Marc "mad" W.
Marc L Abbott
Maria T
Martha Huggins

Maya G Goldstein
Meghan Arcuri
Michele Clemente
Michele Kutner
Nathan Toby
Nicholas Diak
Nicholas Stephenson
Rachel & Jim Larson
Rachel Brune
Randee Dawn
Rebecca E. Hoffman
Reckless Pantalones
Robert Claney
Robert P. Ottone
Sarah
Sasquatch N
Scott Schaper
Scout McLoud
Sherry
Steph Parker
Stephen Ballentine
Steven Van Patten
Tasha Turner
The Creative Fund
Thomas Alan Horne
Timothy DuBois
Venessa Giunta
Victoria Navarra
WD Stancil